# HOLLY'S CHRISTMAS KISS

Holly Michelle Jolly hates Christmas, and she has good reason to. Apart from her ridiculously festive name, tragic and unfortunate events have a habit of happening to her around the holiday season. And this year is no different. After the flight to her once-in-a-lifetime holiday destination is cancelled, she faces the prospect of a cold and lonely Christmas. That is, until she meets Sean Munro. With Sean's help, can she experience her first happy Christmas, or will their meeting just result in more memories she'd rather forget?

ALISON MAY

# HOLLY'S CHRISTMAS KISS

*Complete and Unabridged*

**LINFORD**
*Leicester*

First published in Great Britain in 2016 by
Choc Lit Limited
Surrey

First Linford Edition
published 2018
by arrangement with
Choc Lit Limited
Surrey

A catalogue record for this book is available
from the British Library.

ISBN 978–1–4448–3715–5

Published by
F. A. Thorpe (Publishing)
Anstey, Leicestershire

Set by Words & Graphics Ltd.
Anstey, Leicestershire
Printed and bound in Great Britain by
T. J. International Ltd., Padstow, Cornwall

This book is printed on acid-free paper

*For Paul*

# Acknowledgements

Immense thanks first of all to everyone at Choc Lit, especially to my lovely editor who has held my hand through all three *Christmas Kiss* novellas.

Thanks also to all those lovely people who make writing a less solitary experience — all my RNA, ADC and Pen Club friends, particularly Janet, Lisa and Holly who are always there with wine/cake/sympathy as required.

And finally, thanks, as always, to EngineerBoy for so very many different things.

A special thanks to the Tasting Panel readers who were the first to meet Holly, Cora and Jessica and

made this all possible: Georgie,
Michelle T., Leanne, Sarah A.,
Dorothy, Betty, Jennie H., Isabelle,
Linda Sp., Christie, Jen, Olivia,
Sammi, Nicky, Rosie, Linda G.,
Hrund, Sally C. and Cindy.

# 1

Christmas Eve, 1991

Holly Michelle Jolly

I pretend to be asleep while he fills the pillowcase at the end of my bed. I know it's supposed to be a stocking but Daddy says you don't get enough presents in a stocking, so a pillowcase is better.

I peek out of one eye at him. He's wearing his red suit and he's got a big white beard just like in pictures. He sees me looking. He smiles. 'Ho, ho, ho, Holly,' he says.

I smile back. It's not the really real Santa. I know it's Daddy, but in a way that makes it nicer, because I know the secret. I saw him putting his beard in his briefcase and made him tell me, but he swore me to keep it absolutely top secret so I did. At school Jessica Honeybourne went on and on about how she was going to the big department store to see the real Santa, and I didn't say anything.

He finishes stuffing the presents into the pillowcase.

'Time to sleep now, Holly.'

I nod, and pull the covers up over my head until he's gone. I do definitely try to go to sleep. I screw my eyes up as tight as they'll go and I wait and wait for ages but I'm still awake. It's too exciting. The nearly-Christmasness is building up in my tummy, and it's too much to keep in. It's nearly here. My presents are already here. They're right there at the end of the bed.

I pull the top present out of the pillowcase, just to give it a little shake and a squeeze, but I shake it too hard and it falls on the floor. I climb off the bed to pick it up, scrunching the carpet between my toes as they touch the floor. I can see a little tear in the paper at one end of the parcel. I put it on the bed and stare hard at the tear, trying to open it up with my eyes. It does not work.

I must not open my presents.

I must not open my presents.

I have to wait to open my presents in the morning. I have to wait until it's time to climb into Mummy and Daddy's bed. I look at the clock on my dressing table. It has hands that light up so I can see the time even when it is dark. It is not time yet. It is not even nearly time. I stare at the present again; then I hook my little finger under the tear in the paper and give it a tiny pull. It tears a bit more. I stop.

I must not open my presents.

I give it another little tug. Now the hole is big enough to peek through.

'What are you doing, Holly?' I look round and see my dad standing in the doorway behind me. He's in his pyjamas and dressing gown now, but he still looks like Santa in his eyes.

'Sorry.'

He comes into the room, picks the present up and puts it back in the pillowcase.

'Father Christmas came then?'

I nod, playing along with the game.

'Do you think, maybe we should put this out of reach until morning?'

'Ok.'

He grins. 'Or what if we just took a little peek at this one? It is nearly open.'

I can't believe it. 'Mummy will be cross.'

He winks at me. 'Well I won't tell if you don't.'

I pull the paper off, and find a doll inside. It's a sewed together ragdoll. She's beautiful. I decide she will be my favourite, favourite present, whatever else there is in my pillowcase. Daddy holds her up and then pushes her face against my nose like she's giving me a kiss.

'A dolly for Holly,' he says. Dolly, I think, will be her name forever.

Holly Michelle Jolly smoothed down her bridesmaid dress and surveyed the room. Fairy lights — check. Christmas tree — check. Thick green garland around the bar — check. She shuddered. A wedding reception the week before Christmas. Michelle couldn't remember precisely which circle of hell that was included in, but it was definitely up there on her list of personal horrors; the tinselled gaudiness of Christmas combined with the ridiculous expense of the wedding, and a London wedding at that. Michelle's inner Yorkshire girl flinched when she remembered the price of the miniaturised fish and chip canapés.

Nonetheless, it was, she knew, Jess's dream wedding. They'd spent many an evening over a glass of wine, in their tiny shared flat, planning this event. Even before Jess had met Patrick, her fantasy Christmas wedding had been clear in her mind. And that was the point, after all. It was Michelle's job to make sure everything went perfectly. She swept her gaze across the room again. People seemed to be enjoying themselves. The mulled wine was proving a hit, and the guests were looking increasingly pink and full of cheer. Michelle shook her head, and looked around for her friend. Jess was ensconced with her new groom, both talking to the best man. Michelle's lips pursed, as her gaze settled for a second.

Sean Munro was a friend of Patrick's from years ago when they'd both lived in Edinburgh. Michelle had met him for the first time the day before the wedding, and was not impressed. He was all floppy hair and stupid grins. She'd tried to get him to sit down and go through the schedule for the day, and he'd tried to get her to put a whole mince pie in her mouth in one go. Michelle had had to explain, quite firmly, that they were here to make sure everything ran smoothly for the happy couple. They were not here to have fun. He hadn't taken her seriously. She had found her carefully typed and bullet pointed list of things he needed to attend to 'On The Day' dropped by his chair after he left.

Michelle glanced at her watch. It was nearly eight. Evening canapés were supposed to be delivered punctually at 7.45 p.m., but there wasn't a white-shirted tray-bearer to be seen. Michelle sighed and set off to find someone to scold before Jess noticed the problem.

\* \* \*

'So am I supposed to dance with a bridesmaid or something? That's a best man thing? Right?'

Sean Munro was leaning on the bar, booted and kilted, watching the guests shake, shimmy and sway as the band played *Santa Baby* for about the eighteenth time. He took a sip from his mulled wine and grinned at the bride. She shook her head.

'Michelle's not really the dancing sort.'

He looked around, finding himself hoping that he'd spot Jess's bossy bridesmaid.

'Where is she anyway? I've not had a chance to talk to her.'

'I'm not sure.' Jess turned her head, expensively sculpted bridal hairstyle and all, to scan the room for her friend's distinctive red hair. 'Probably fixing something on my behalf.'

Sean smiled. 'Well, I didn't get these knees out for nothing. If I can't dance with a bridesmaid, I'm dancing with the bride!'

He dragged her onto the dance floor, and spun her round and round. Innocent bydancers were scattered from their path, as Sean twirled his partner with more enthusiasm and gusto than expertise, until the groom decided it was time to rescue his new wife.

'You're gonna do someone a damage mate.' Patrick detached Jess from his friend's exertions. 'Find your own girl to fling about the place.'

Jess took a second to regain her breath before joining in. 'Quite right. I'm sure we can find you a nice girl somewhere amongst my friends.'

Patrick laughed. 'This time next year. Back in your kilt. Doing one of your weird Scottish dances with your new bride?'

Sean felt his face tense but he didn't reply beyond a small shake of his head. He could feel Patrick looking at him with customary concern. They'd been friends since what Sean still thought of as his 'Lost Months', living in Edinburgh straight after 'The Breakup', and Patrick remained on the lookout for a return to those moods, no matter how many times Sean pointed out that the best part of a decade had passed. The silence sat in the middle of the group for slightly longer than was comfortable.

Patrick turned to his bride. 'So, how

about a dance with me? A slower dance?'

Jess nodded, and the pair stepped back onto the floor. Sean watched them. He was actually enjoying the wedding. It was several orders of bridal magazine magnitude removed from his own tiny registry office affair. On the dance floor, the happy couple turned and swayed, wrapped in each other's arms. There was something exclusive about their togetherness. You could see, right in that moment, that they only needed one another. Sean turned away.

Across the room something else caught his eye, and lifted his spirits. He walked over to the huge Christmas tree and appraised it. Not dropping much, but you'd expect that with a Nordmann fir. Nice shape. Tall. He wondered how much the hotel had paid for it. The decorations were corporate-classy. Not the right approach, in Sean's opinion. Tree decorations should be personal and have stories attached to them. This was a bit too tidy for his liking. He glanced upwards and realised he was standing beneath a large sprig of mistletoe. His habitual good humour cooled a little. Such a waste.

He turned to walk back towards the dance floor.

And it happened.

A body crashed into his, as he turned without looking. He put out his hands to support the elusive non-dancing bridesmaid who was momentarily pressed against him. His fingers brushed against satin covering soft flesh. His nostrils were filled with the scent of the shampoo from her thick red hair. He blinked. Michelle rested against his body for a second and then staggered backwards, pushing her hand onto his chest for balance.

'I'm sorry.' She stood up straight. 'Sorry.'

'Are you Ok?'

'I'm fine.' She gestured vaguely towards the bar. 'I have things to see to.'

He paused, but only for a second,

before he jumped in. 'But you owe me a kiss.'

Sean surprised himself. He looked at the woman in front of him again. Long wavy red hair, pale white skin, bright blue eyes. Something unfamiliar started to stir in the back of his mind. He flicked his eyes upwards towards the beam, which supported the large sprig of mistletoe directly above them.

'Who put that there?' she said.

'What?'

She was frowning. 'There was only supposed to be mistletoe over Jess and Patrick's seats at the top table.'

She glared at the offending decoration, as if the mistletoe had placed itself on the beam with the express purpose of annoying her.

'What does it matter who put it there? It's Christmas.'

'It's not Christmas for another three days.'

'It's near enough. We're under the mistletoe. It's probably bad luck or something not to kiss.' He grinned at her, a soft playful grin that felt strange to him, like something from a different age.

'Bad luck?' He watched Michelle's expression switch from irritation to incredulity. 'What about all the horrid diseases you can catch from kissing?'

Bit harsh, Sean thought. 'I don't have any horrible diseases.'

She shook her head. 'Well I might have. You barely know me.'

Sean grinned again. 'I'll take my chances. I don't have a choice. We're standing under mistletoe. We'd be breaking an important law of Christmas.'

'There's no such thing as a law of Christmas.'

'Of course there is. There's loads of things you have to do at Christmas.' Sean sensed he wasn't winning the argument. 'Well maybe it's not an actual law. Strong convention. We'd be breaking a strong convention of Christmas.'

'Go on! Kiss him!' Jess's voice carried

over the music from the edge of the dance floor. Michelle glared at her friend, and sighed.

'Fine.' She lifted her face and puckered her lips.

Sean bent his head to meet her. Without thinking he moved his hand towards her cheek as their lips edged closer. The scent of her skin, the sound of her breath, the warmth of her body, started to play on his senses. He leaned forward, just a fraction more. He was a moment away from her lips. Just one moment.

Crash.

She jumped away from him at the sound. At the far side of the dance floor a waiter slipped and dropped a perfectly balanced tray of canapés to the floor. Michelle pointed in the direction of the unfortunate waiter. 'I'd better go and . . . '

Sean watched her stride away. She was all the way across the room before he noticed that he was holding his breath. Slowly, he exhaled.

## Two days before Christmas, 2013

Michelle's taxi drew up to the drop-off point at Heathrow Airport. Snow was starting to fall as she paid the driver and stepped out onto the pavement. Michelle shivered. She'd always hated winter. Right from the point, usually sometime in the middle of October, when the first person gestured towards the darkening sky and told her it was starting to look Christmassy, she could happily avoid the whole season. Given the option, Michelle thought, she'd probably prefer to hibernate until spring. The thought that this time tomorrow she'd be sipping a cocktail on the beach in the Cayman Islands was the only thing keeping her from jumping straight back into the cab and demanding a ride to the nearest place with central heating.

Her case seemed to have got heavier since she left the hotel. By the time she'd navigated her way to the right check-in area she was sweating despite the cold. Waiting in the queue, she unwrapped her scarf from around her neck and started to undo her heavy duffle coat. At least once she was on the plane she wouldn't have to put those back on for another two weeks.

The doubt she'd been fighting, ever since she'd clicked 'Book' on the online travel site, popped back into her head. It was so much money. Could she really justify it when she spent her working life telling her clients not to overspend? She swallowed. It was what her mother had wanted. A small inheritance, not much once the funeral was paid for, but enough to allow Michelle to take the holiday of a lifetime. That was what her mother, quite uncharacteristically, had instructed her to do, and it was up to Michelle to ensure that it was worth every penny.

With her coat balanced on top of her suitcase she took a moment to look around. The queue for check-in was nearly all adults. The Caribbean at Christmas must be a preference of those without young families. She glanced around again. The queue was also exclusively couples, apart from Michelle. She stood up straight. There was no shame in going on holiday alone. In fact, she'd probably have a better time than all these women with boyfriends or husbands in tow. She wouldn't be worrying about making someone else happy.

Michelle spent the whole year sorting out other people's problems: planning Jess's wedding; helping Jess move; running around after her boss; running around after her clients. She remembered her mother's instructions: 'Put yourself first, Michelle.' That was the plan.

The couple in front of her embarked on a sloppy and prolonged kiss. Michelle looked away, decidedly ignoring the memory rushing into her mind of a moment that got away. She was definitely better off on her own.

The queue inched forward, until Michelle was called in front of a smiling check-in assistant with tinsel pinned to her uniform and reindeer antlers on her head.

'Merry Christmas!'

Michelle didn't reply. It might be nearly Christmas. That didn't mean she had to pander to the fact. She lifted her bag onto the conveyer and held her ticket and passport out to the assistant.

'Thank you, Miss . . . ' The woman glanced down at the passport. ' . . . Jolly! Oooh, how festive!'

Yeah. Nothing beat being called Jolly at Christmastime. She caught the check-in woman looking at her full name. Holly Michelle Jolly. She could see that another set of jokes she'd heard a thousand times before were already forming in the woman's mind.

'I use Michelle.'

The woman suppressed a smirk. 'Did you pack this bag yourself Miss Jolly?'

'Yes.'

'And has anyone asked you to take any items on the flight with you?' The girl asked the question by rote, in the sing-song voice of someone so used to saying the words that they'd forgotten the meaning a long time ago.

Michelle shook her head.

'Excellent. Window or aisle?'

Michelle paused. She did prefer a window seat. She remembered the one time she'd been on an aeroplane with her dad, and how he'd let her take the window seat. She'd been transfixed by the sight of the clouds drifting below them. Knowing her luck though, she'd get sat next to someone who'd stink to high heaven, regale her with stories of what they'd got up to at their office Christmas party, and then fall fast asleep for the next seven hours, leaving her pinned in her seat. Aisle would mean she could get up and stretch her legs. She didn't want to risk a deep vein thrombosis.

'Aisle, please.'

The assistant tapped a few keys, before another thought struck Michelle. She remembered a documentary she'd watched about plane crashes, and how to survive them.

'And within seven rows of an exit.'

The woman raised an eyebrow, and tapped the keys some more. Eventually the boarding pass printed out.

'You'll be boarding around a quarter to three. We don't have a gate yet, but if you go through security and watch the monitors, it'll come up about thirty minutes before we board.'

'Thank you.' Michelle took the boarding pass and her passport from the assistant and turned away.

'Thank you, madam. Merry Christmas!'

Michelle suppressed a grimace. Hopefully, once she got to Grand Cayman, people would be more relaxed and not quite so irritatingly perky.

The queue for security was more suited to Michelle's mood. By this stage, people were tired of waiting, and the ritual of removing jewellery, belts and wristwatches was being completed with bored faces and a refreshing lack of festive cheer.

Michelle stuffed her coat and belt into a plastic tray and put the rucksack she was carrying as hand baggage onto the conveyer. She walked through the bodyscan, only to hear the machine bleep. The security guard stepped forward and gestured her back through the scanner. She emptied her pockets fully, and removed the plain gold studs from her ears before walking back through the contraption.

The machine bleeped again and the red light flashed above her head. Michelle followed the guard's instructions to stand with her arms outstretched and legs apart. The woman flicked a handheld device over Michelle's body. Michelle's face flushed red. She knew this was a perfectly everyday occurrence, but she couldn't help but feel that people were staring at her.

The security guard checked with a colleague and then smiled at Michelle.

'Ok. No problem. On you go.'

Michelle dropped her arms. She didn't want to have to go through all this on the way home. 'What set it off?'

The guard shrugged. 'Sometimes it just goes off. You're fine.'

Michelle didn't consider that a satisfactory answer, but the guard had moved on to wave her detector at some other poor innocent. Michelle started to collect her belongings from the tray.

'You managed to talk your way out of that one then?'

The distinctive Scottish accent made her stop dead. She turned round slowly to see Sean Munro smirking at her. Her eyes were drawn straight to his mouth, to those inviting lips that . . . She shook her head and forced her gaze away from his face.

'You're not wearing your kilt.' She blurted the words as her glance dropped to his legs.

'No.'

What was she saying? Of course he wasn't wearing a kilt. Just because he wore a kilt in her imagination, didn't mean he always wore a kilt. Not that she'd been imagining Sean. She was tired, she decided, and flustered from the security check. Yes. Flustered. It would pass.

'What are you doing here?' He obviously had no right to be here. This was her holiday. She was supposed to be getting away from any distractions.

The smirk extended into a grin, 'Don't pretend you're not pleased to see me.'

Michelle took a breath. She'd simply run into an acquaintance. They would exchange the time of day and go their separate ways. There was no reason to be getting worked up. His deep green eyes weren't a reason. The slight crumple to the T-shirt he was wearing wasn't a reason. The flash of tight muscled torso she glimpsed as Sean rubbed his hand over the back of his neck wasn't a reason. The warm intoxicating smell as he leant towards her definitely wasn't a reason to lose her composure. Wait a minute. He was leaning towards her.

Michelle stepped sideways, away from the heat of Sean's body. He lifted her rucksack off the table and swung it over his shoulder, raising his eyebrow slightly at her jump to the side.

'But, what are you doing here?' Michelle spluttered out the question again.

'I'm catching a plane.'

'Yes.' Well, obviously. 'A plane to?'

'Home for Christmas.'

'Home?' Of course home. That's where people went for Christmas, wasn't it? They spent it with family. They had traditions, and customs that they shared with their parents and passed on to their children. Was that what Sean's Christmas would be like? Michelle swallowed the thought.

Sean was still talking. ' . . . near Edinburgh.'

Michelle nodded, hoping she hadn't missed anything important.

'Are you heading home too?'

Michelle shook her head. There wasn't really a home to head to any more. Her mother had passed away. And her father was . . . well, her father was not somebody she would choose to spend her holidays with.

'To the Caribbean. On holiday.'

'Who with?'

'Just me.'

'At Christmas?'

The hint of concern in Sean's voice made the muscles in Michelle's neck twitch. 'What's wrong with that?'

'Nothing.' He regrouped quickly. 'When's your flight?'

She paused and took a breath. 'Three.'

Sean nodded and started striding away from the security area and into the main departure lounge. Michelle scurried to keep up with his longer legs.

'So, what do you fancy?'

What do you fancy? Michelle opened and closed her mouth with no sound. What did she fancy? She gave up. The less she said the less likely it was that she'd see the teasing grin reappear at Sean's lips.

He gestured towards the large, fluorescent-lit store in front of them. 'We could see how many perfumes they'll let us test before they realise we're not buying.'

Michelle shook her head. It was a ridiculous thing for a grown man to suggest.

Sean glanced around, and pointed at a coffee shop. 'Hot chocolate? We could get cream and marshmallows and see if we can drink it without getting cream on our noses?'

Hot chocolate had always been what her dad would bring Michelle if she caught a cold. She had a picture in her head of him sitting on the edge of her bed with a big steaming mug for each of them. If Mum was out he'd buy the synthetic cream in an aerosol can and spray that on top. If Mum was around she would shout at him for daring to bring aerosol cream into her kitchen.

Apart from at Christmas. At Christmas, she used to let him have his way. That was a very long time ago, but Michelle could taste the memory of the cheap sugary cream dissolving on her tongue. She smiled.

Sean returned the smile. 'So hot chocolate?'

'No, thank you.' This holiday was about time alone, not about playing like children with a man who was old enough to know better. 'Can I have my bag please?'

Sean placed the rucksack strap into her outstretched hand.

'Thank you. Now, if you don't mind, I'd rather be on my own. I'll be quite happy reading my book.'

His eyebrows rose slightly, but the smile didn't leave his lips. 'If that's what you'd prefer.'

Michelle adopted a light tone. There was no reason not to be cordial. 'Have a nice Christmas.'

★　★　★

Sean didn't move as she walked away. He'd met this woman twice now. This time he'd even made her smile, but both times he'd ended up watching her leave. It wasn't a situation he was used to. If Sean was honest, in recent years he'd tended to be the one doing the walking away. It was safer that way.

It seemed a shame, though, Michelle holidaying alone at Christmas. He let the thought settle in his brain. Even during his lowest moments, Sean couldn't imagine spending Christmas away from his family and friends. That was it. He felt sorry for her being alone. Obviously if she'd told him she was flying out to meet a boyfriend he would have been fine with that. Completely fine.

Sean wandered without much intent around the departure lounge duty free stores. He remembered the first time he'd flown from Edinburgh to London, back before travelling for work had been part and parcel of his life. He'd been a twenty-year-old farm boy who'd never boarded a plane before. He remembered the shops at Edinburgh's airport. Aisles and aisles of perfume, scotch whisky, books, scarves, jewellery, and bags, all potential gifts for his hostess. In the end he'd plumped for perfume. A bottle of he didn't remember what, a tiny bottle, but much bigger than he could afford at the time. The assistant had smirked, and told him it was the perfect scent to get a young girl to fall in love with him. Maybe that had been his mistake all those years ago. He didn't ask what would be the perfect scent to persuade a girl who'd fallen out of love with him to change her mind.

His phone pinged in his pocket. He took it out and glanced at the screen. A new text. He rolled his eyes at the name. Speak of the devil and he will appear. That was the saying, wasn't it? Cora went one better. You only had to think of her and she popped up.

The text was breezy and flirtatious in tone. What part of no didn't she understand? Sean paused as he read the end of the message. 'Hope to see you over Christmas.' She must think he was staying in London. No chance. He'd be safely in Scotland, and he couldn't imagine Cora gracing the ancestral home with her presence for the holidays. She would, no doubt, have a much more glamorous option lined up.

# 2

## Christmas Day, 1996

### Sean

Mum's wielding her pudding ladle.

'Who's for seconds?'

Bel shakes her head. She never has seconds, because she's watching her figure. I don't know what she thinks is going to happen to it. I shake my head too. It's twenty to three already. There isn't time for seconds. Nobody else seems to care. The rest of the family dig in. I push my chair back from the table.

'Where do you think you're going?'

'Out for a bit.'

Dad shakes his head. 'Not until everyone's finished.'

It's not fair. Now I have to sit here and I don't get any more pudding. And old people eat so slowly. Granddad's the worst. His teeth don't fit properly, so he can't really chew. I have to sit and listen to every gummy mouthful. Eventually he puts down his spoon.

'I'm going out for a bit.' I dash up to my room and grab the present from my drawer, and then I'm out of the house, across the yard, and through the first field at a run. I scale the gate into the second field and start to slow down. I want to get my breath back before I see her. After Christmas, we're definitely going to tell people. Then I'll be able to walk up to her front door like normal. I climb over the far fence, into the next field, and onto the Strachan estate.

She's waiting at the edge of the field, arms wrapped across her body, and scarf pulled up to her ears. I stuff my hands in my pockets and drop my head.

'All right.'

'Hi.' She's got her eyes down to the floor, but she looks up at me through her lashes. 'I thought you weren't coming.'

'Dad made me stay 'til everyone had

finished dinner. I'm probably gonna get bollocked anyway for not helping wash up.'

She wrinkles her nose, probably at the idea of having to do chores. 'Did you tell them where you were going?'

I shake my head.

'Cool.'

'They wouldn't mind. Bel's boyfriend stays over all the time.'

'She's older than you.'

'Not much.'

She shakes her head. 'Mine'd go mental.'

'Why?'

'Cause they're stupid.'

I'm pissed off now. 'They think I'm too rough for you.'

'It's stupid.' She doesn't deny it though.

I look across the fields to Cora's house. It's big and it's modern. My dad calls it a bloody eyesore, but that's just because he's not used to buildings that aren't held together with duct tape.

Cora takes a step towards me. 'Don't be grumpy.'

She reaches her arms up around my neck. 'It's more fun this way anyhow. Sneaking about.'

She presses her body against mine. 'It's sexy.'

She's got round me. She always does. I slide my arms around her waist and squeeze her bum through the layers.

She smiles. 'So where's my pressie?'

# 3

Two days before Christmas, 2013

Michelle found a seat, wedged between a Chinese family and a man fast asleep across two chairs and a table, at one end of the departure lounge and tried to calm her breathing. Resting her hands on her lap, she realised that she was shaking slightly. What was happening to her? She hoped that she wasn't coming down with some sort of virus that would mean a holiday wasted tucked up in her hotel room.

A battered pair of Converse at the bottom of a pair of denim-clad legs was heading towards her. She looked up and offered a half smile. The stranger nodded a little uncertainly and carried on. She dropped her head. It wasn't Sean. Of course, it wasn't Sean. There were probably thousands of people in the terminal. Not all the men wearing jeans would be Sean. And she wasn't interested if it was. Sean Munro, so far as Michelle could tell, was an immature little kid trapped in a grown-up body. She'd seen him twirling Jess around the dance floor like a maniac, and he was no better today, talking about getting cream on his nose and suggesting playing pranks in shops.

She tried to focus on her book, struggling through a couple of unengrossing chapters. She wriggled in the hard angular seat. Time crawled by. She glanced at her watch; it was half past two. Her flight would be boarding soon, and she'd be on her way. She looked up at the departure board. The screen was full of the dreaded word: DELAYED. She scanned down the list for her flight: 'Wait In Lounge.' She sighed with relief. The idea of a long delay didn't appeal one little bit.

Twenty minutes later, the display was still flashing, 'Wait In Lounge.'

Michelle closed the book she was hardly reading anyway. Surely, they would be boarding soon. Either way, she needed to stretch her legs. She stuffed the book into the top of her rucksack and picked up her bag. As she stood up, she was taken aback by how stiff she'd got, sitting on the hard seat for so long. She walked slowly across the lounge and turned a corner. In front of her was a full floor to ceiling window with an uninterrupted view of the runway. On a normal day this would be the ideal spot to watch the planes taking off from one of the busiest airports on the planet. Today there was no such view.

Michelle walked up to the window and placed her hand against the glass. The runway was silent. Nothing was moving apart from the snowflakes which danced and fell in front of her, creating a cover of white across the ground. She turned back towards the departure lounge, looking out for a display board.

## 15:10 BA345 Grand Cayman
## DELAYED.

It really was just her luck. Her first proper holiday in more than twelve years, and her flight was delayed. She blinked hard. No point getting down-hearted about it. The only sensible thing to do was go back to her seat and wait.

She made her way, more briskly now, back across the main lounge, and saw that her earlier seat had been taken. Searching the departures hall she couldn't see an available place to sit. She walked in between the rows of chairs, clambering over bags, push-chairs and people's legs. There wasn't a single seat free. Eventually she dragged her rucksack back to the window overlooking the runway, dumped it down on the floor and tried to get comfortable sitting on her bag. It was not a dream start to her dream holiday.

The time passed slowly, too slowly. Michelle shifted around, trying to find a comfortable position on the cold floor. She read for a bit, looked out of the window for a bit, closed her eyes for a bit trying to rest. As the ache in her back grew, she silently cursed her mother for forcing her into this holiday. The money would have been put to far better use invested in her ISA, or topping up her pension pot.

Outside the snow continued to fall. Michelle shifted and stretched to get a view of an information board. Her flight was still listed as DELAYED. She scanned for details of the Edinburgh flight. It wasn't on the board. She glanced at her watch. Nearly five o'clock. Sean must be on his way already. An unfamiliar feeling crept into her tummy. Disappointment? Michelle told herself not to be so silly. She settled, as best she could, back onto the floor, trying to use her rucksack as a pillow. She gazed out of the window. A thickening white layer was covering the runway, crying out for a child in wellingtons to jump full-footed into the unspoilt snow. It was a silly thought, and it made Michelle shake her head. Jumping in snow was just the sort of frivolity that she could do without; every bit as foolish in its own way as spending your last few pounds on a present that would hardly get played with, or a turkey that would barely fit in the oven. She remembered her father bringing home a turkey on Christmas Eve and her mother complaining that it was too big, and she remembered eating turkey soup and turkey fritters long into January. At least her mother understood how to plan ahead.

'I bought you a hot chocolate, just in case.'

The voice interrupted her thoughts, and Michelle tried, unsuccessfully, to scramble to her feet. She ended up half kneeling, half squatting, eyes level with Sean's crotch, her hair halfway out of its ponytail and sticking to her face.

'I thought you'd gone.' She tilted her head towards his face and decided to carry on as if this was a quite normal position for chit-chat. 'Your flight's not on the board.'

Sean smiled. 'You noticed.'

'Well, I was, I didn't particularly . . . ' Michelle let her voice trail off. She'd noticed, and now he knew she'd noticed. She wished she hadn't said anything.

Sean held out his hand and Michelle let him help her to her feet. The touch sent tingles through her body. She dropped his hand and tried to regain her composure. Sean wasn't her type. She liked men who were put together, not ones who looked like they'd fallen into their clothes by happy accident.

He held the hot chocolate towards her. 'It's got cream and marshmallows, but I suppose you can keep the lid on if you don't want cream on your nose.'

She took the drink from him, realising that she'd arrived at the airport nearly five hours ago and not had anything to eat or drink since. She kept her gaze firmly towards the floor, or at best Sean's shoes. Calm and

41

under control was her new mantra. 'Thank you.'

'You're welcome.'

Michelle felt herself smiling. That was probably the first bit of normal conversation they'd managed. She swallowed, raised her head and met Sean's gaze.

He nodded towards the snowy scene outside the window. 'My flight was cancelled.'

'Oh no! I'm sorry.' She put her hand out to touch his arm in sympathy, but pulled it back before her fingers made contact. There was really no need for any more touching. 'What are you going to do?'

He shrugged. 'Stand here. Drink my hot chocolate. Watch the snow. What about you?'

'Well, my flight's only delayed. I'm still going . . . ' Her voice trailed off as she saw Sean's eyebrows flick up.

'I'm sorry. I don't think anyone's flying out of here today.'

'It still says delayed.' She looked

forlornly at the departures board and then back out through the window. The snow was still falling, covering the scene outside in an ever-deepening blanket of white.

He paused as if deciding what to say next. Eventually he smiled softly. 'All right. I guess we'd better make ourselves comfortable for the wait then.'

'We?' Michelle could hear the horror in her own voice. Sean, however, seemed to be immune, or, at the very least, choosing to ignore it. He had put his own drink down, taken off his jacket and laid it out across the floor.

'Madam,' he took Michelle's drink out of her hand and gestured toward the coat. 'Hardly the full Walter Raleigh, but the best I can do.'

He nodded back towards the main departure lounge. 'There's not a seat to be had through there.'

'But you don't have to wait. Your flight's cancelled. You can go home.'

'And leave you all alone? Never.'

'Why are you still here?'

'There is nowhere I would rather be.'

Well that made no sense. What was the point in hanging around at an airport after your flight had been cancelled? Michelle opened her mouth to argue, but stopped herself. Bringing her a drink had been kind. She should probably try to be gracious. Very slowly, she lowered herself onto the coat and wriggled to one side, leaving space for Sean to sit beside her.

He sat himself down and picked up his hot chocolate. He pulled the plastic lid off, and took a generous gulp, allowing the cream to settle on his top lip and the tip of his nose. Turning his face towards Michelle he grinned and raised his eyebrows in challenge.

'Don't be silly.'

'Why not?' He looked disappointed, but wiped the cream from his nose and lip with the back of his hand.

'Because you're a grown-up, not an eight-year-old.'

'No. It's Christmas. Everyone gets to act like a kid at Christmas.'

'Don't be stupid.'

'Why not? Nothing wrong with embracing your inner eight-year-old.'

Michelle rolled her eyes. 'Apart from that it's completely unrealistic. I have a grown-up life, a grown-up flat, a grown-up job.'

'What do you do?'

'I'm a money adviser.'

Sean rolled his eyes. 'Like in a bank?'

Michelle shook her head vigorously. In her line of work, banks were usually on the opposite side of the argument. 'I'm a debt adviser. I help people who can't cope with their debts.'

Sean laughed. 'Figures.'

'What?' There was something about his tone that Michelle didn't care for.

'Jess said you were always trying to fix things for everyone, you know, make everything better.'

'What's wrong with that?'

'Nothing.' Sean shook his head. 'Seriously, nothing. But wouldn't it be nice to take a break from being sensible?'

What a preposterous idea. It was just the sort of thing Michelle fancied her father would think. She closed the door on the thought before it had chance to take hold.

'You can't take time off from being grown-up.'

Sean considered her answer in silence. 'What about running away to the Caribbean for Christmas? That's taking a break.'

'Not from being responsible.' Michelle's voice raised. She twisted uncomfortably to face Sean. 'This holiday is all about taking responsibility for myself, not needing someone else to look after me.'

Sean raised his hands in submission. 'Sorry.'

They fell into silence. After talking about the importance of being grown-up she realised that refusing to let it go would look childish. Beaten by her own argument. She swallowed the warm creamy chocolate and let out a breath. 'It's Ok.'

They sat for a moment looking out at the white landscape beyond the window.

'Excuse me madam.' Michelle turned around and saw a young woman in airline uniform approaching them from behind, clutching a clipboard.

The woman gestured towards the airline insignia on her jacket. 'Can I ask if you're booked on a flight with us today?'

Michelle nodded.

'Can I ask your name?'

'Michelle Jolly.'

'Oh! Very festive.' The woman smiled the smile of a person who knows that they get to go home at the end of the day. Michelle glowered. 'And, can I ask which flight you're booked on?'

'Grand Cayman.'

'I'm terribly sorry. That flight has been cancelled today.' The woman flicked through the pages on her clipboard to avoid eye contact.

Michelle sighed in disbelief. Obviously she could see the snowbound runway, but she'd been telling herself that somehow her flight would be different.

Next to her, Sean scrambled to his feet. 'And is it being rescheduled?'

The woman glanced back at her clipboard. 'And you are?'

'Sean Munro.'

'And are you booked on the same flight?' Her eyes were scanning the clipboard as she spoke.

Sean shook his head. 'I'm just a friend.'

'All right,' she replied, in a tone that implied that friends weren't really all right, but would be tolerated in these unusual circumstances. 'The flight will be rescheduled.'

Michelle's mood brightened and she dragged herself to her feet. So she could stay in an airport hotel tonight, and fly tomorrow. Yes, her holiday would be a day shorter but it wasn't the end of the world. The woman was still talking.

' . . . so you see, with the forecast as it is, and Christmas, and our aircrews are all over the place, that's really the best we can do.'

'What is?'

'The twenty-seventh. We should be all back to normal by then.' The woman smiled brightly but without sincerity. 'Maybe the twenty-eighth.'

Michelle was dismayed. The twenty-eighth of December. That would be five days off her holiday, and, even worse, she was stuck in the UK for Christmas.

'But, I've booked a hotel and all the money . . . '

Her half-formed thought was met with another disengaged smile and a sheet of paper pulled from the woman's clipboard. 'For financial compensation, refunds and any other complaints, you'll need to fill in this form, and return it to the address at the top. Merry Christmas!'

The woman hurried away, as if too much talk of refunds and complaints might dent her brittle cheerful shell.

Michelle turned to Sean and for a second her bottom lip trembled, before she snapped her usual brisk exterior back in place. 'Oh well, no point hanging around here.'

Sean looked momentarily confused. 'No. I suppose not. So are you going to head home?'

Michelle nodded. 'Not much else to do.'

She held her hand out in front of her. 'Thank you for the hot chocolate.'

He shook her hand uncertainly. 'No problem. You don't want to share a cab or anything?'

'No thank you. I'll be fine from here.' Because nothing had changed. This Christmas was about independence. Chance meetings and almost-kisses didn't mean anything. She picked up her rucksack and walked briskly into the crowded departure hall.

★ ★ ★

Sean watched her leave, before collecting his own jacket and bag, and tossing the empty hot chocolate cups into the

50

bin. Why had he waited with her anyway? He could have been well on the way to Edinburgh by now. He was behaving like the old Sean. He'd sworn off acting on impulse a long time ago.

He glanced at his watch. If he managed to find a cab, he probably had enough time to get back into London and catch the sleeper train north, if there was space, and if everyone else who was on his flight hadn't left with the same idea hours earlier. He rubbed his eyes. At the moment it wasn't just the best plan; it was the only plan.

He jogged across the departure hall, jumping and jostling to get past the crowds of people berating the airline staff. He resisted a smile at the sight of the woman who'd spoken to him and Michelle looking significantly less bright and festive. Partway across the room he realised that he had no idea where he was going. The whole layout of the airport was designed to stop people leaving from the departures area. Once you were through security, you were supposed to leave on a plane.

He stopped and looked around. The bright festive woman was peeling herself away from another group of disgruntled looking passengers.

'Excuse me.'

'Yes?' The smile snapped back onto her face, but it wasn't quite as glossy as it had been earlier.

Sean beamed at her. 'Tough day?'

She fluttered her eyelids slightly in the full wattage of his smile. 'Well, you know . . . '

'Sure. Look . . . ' he glanced for a name badge but found none. 'I was wondering if you could help me get out of here?'

'Oh. Yes.' The woman pointed towards an escalator at the far end of the hall. 'If you go up there and follow the corridor round, they've opened up the doors through to Arrivals.'

Sean grinned again. 'Thank you. Happy Christmas.'

'Yes.' The brightness was returning with vigour, and she shouted a festive greeting at Sean's departing back. 'Merry Christmas!'

Sean resumed his half-run, half-leap across the bustling hall and jogged up the escalator two steps at a time. The corridor upstairs was quieter. It didn't seem like many people had worked out how to get out of the departure lounge yet.

Sean followed the signs to Arrivals, and came out at a junction with signposts to 'Baggage Reclaim' and 'Buses and Taxis.' He followed the Baggage Reclaim sign and saw his case circling on the nearest carousel. So that was one benefit of hanging around at the airport for an hour after your flight was cancelled — no wait for your baggage. He grabbed his case and bounded towards the sliding doors to the outside world. The cold outside air hit him in a blast. He pulled his jacket tight around him and fastened the zip, but it wasn't the cold that made him stop. It was the quiet.

He'd been visiting London most of his adult life and was a regular through

Heathrow. He couldn't remember seeing the arrivals area so quiet. It made sense. If there were no planes taking off, presumably there weren't any landing either. And if there were no planes coming in, then Arrivals would be deserted. Hardly any cars coming and going. A few people milling around, waiting for buses. Only two taxis waiting at the rank. And what noise there was, was being deadened by the soft floating fall of the snow. In the middle of an international airport, in one of the busiest cities in the world, he had managed to stumble into a truly silent night.

Sean smiled. Despite the flight being cancelled, and his day being a huge mess, he could feel the stirrings of Christmas excitement in his gut, exactly the same as when he was a kid seeing the first decorations going up or spying the tins of biscuits and treats stowed away on top of the kitchen cupboard waiting for Christmas to officially begin. He grinned and walked towards the first of the taxis.

Michelle waited at baggage reclaim. Seriously, how long could it take for one bag to come through? It wasn't as if they had to unload it from the aeroplane hold. So far as she could work out, the luggage had never got that far, but still she was stuck here waiting for her suitcase to re-emerge from the bowels of the airport. Slowly the baggage hall started to fill up with miserable faces. Parents alternately bickering and placating fractious children. Couples standing in strained, disappointed silence. Airline staff with clipboards looking harassed and tired. People on their phones trying to beg rooms for the night and lifts home from the airport.

That made Michelle think. At least she knew she had somewhere to stay over Christmas. Of course, Jess would be looking forward to her first Christmas with her shiny new husband, but Michelle was sure she'd be more than welcome once she explained her predicament. She started to brighten. It might even be fun. She could help with the cooking. Having another pair of hands would be useful anyway.

She walked a few feet away from the crowd and pulled her phone out of her pocket. She hit Jess's number on her speed-dial. It rang for a few moments before she answered.

'Hiya. Are you there already?'

Michelle had to think for a moment before she remembered where she was supposed to be.

'Er no. Not exactly. They've cancelled my flight. I'm not going after all.'

'Oh no.' Her voice was full of concern. 'What are you going to do?'

'Well, I was wondering if I could stay with you, just over Christmas . . . ' She stopped, waiting to hear Jess's assent.

Her friend paused. It wasn't a long pause, but it was enough. 'I'm sure you can. That'll be fine.'

Jess drifted into silence. Michelle could hear Patrick talking away from the phone. His voice was light, happy, intimate. Michelle's image of herself cooking a perfect Christmas dinner fractured in her mind. This was their time to do things like that together. Michelle would be an intruder in their blissful little bubble.

'Actually, I might head back to Leeds.'

'Oh. Are you sure?' Jess sounded surprised, but not disappointed.

'Yeah. Some people had invited me over on Boxing Day, and Christmas Day on my own might be nice.'

'Oh. Ok.' She didn't try to talk her out of it, which only served to confirm that it was the right decision.

'Yeah. Have a good Christmas.' Michelle fought to keep the crack out of her voice.

'You too.'

'Ok then. Good . . . ' Click. Jess hung up.

Michelle turned back towards the baggage carousel. The carousel at the far end of the hall seemed to be slowly creaking into life. This was fine. She would collect her bag, get a bus or the tube to King's Cross station and head back to Leeds. Christmas was just one day after all, so spending it on her own would be fine. It was what she'd planned. All her books could still be read. It would be big jumpers and pots of tea, rather than bikinis and cocktails.

She made her way through the bodies lined up around the baggage carousel. Her suitcase was one of the first to come through, and she hauled it off the belt and started to fight her way back through the throng. Her eyes were stinging slightly, but she refused to allow herself to cry. Michelle Jolly did not cry.

No flight. No one to spend Christmas with. She looked at her watch. Would it be too late for the train by the time she'd made it to King's Cross? She added the fact that she had nowhere to stay tonight to her list of things she absolutely wasn't going to get upset about, and tugged at her bag. Her muscles strained from the exertion after lying on the hard floor.

She paused before the double doors that led out to the bus stops to put her scarf back on and button her coat. So much for two weeks of guaranteed sunny weather. The cold air stung her cheeks and she could feel the tears starting to well up. They weren't proper tears, she decided, just her eyes watering from the cold.

Michelle gave herself a stern talking to in her head. She hadn't cried when Jess moved out of their shared Leeds flat to come to London, even though Jess had been in a flood. She hadn't cried when Mum had forbidden her from attending her half-brother's Christmastime christening service. She hadn't even cried at her mum's funeral. She wasn't going to cry because she was stuck on her own in the cold.

Bundled up in her duffle coat, and with her scarf pulled around her head, Michelle dragged her suitcase towards the bus stops. At the first shelter she stopped and read the sign. Of course, it didn't help. She didn't know where she was going, so she had no idea which bus to get. Had she missed the last train? Should she head to the railway station and try to sleep there and catch an early train in the morning, or should she look for a hotel? Would all the airport hotels be full with so many flights cancelled? Should she really be paying out for a night in a hotel, when she was at risk of losing so much money on her holiday already? Maybe she should have stayed put in the departures hall. At least it was warm in there.

All at once, the decisions overwhelmed her, and she felt the proper tears start to fall. Fat, salty, gulpy tears poured down her face and she cried, for the first time she could remember, in a public place. It was humiliating, and the realisation that it was humiliating made her cry more. Michelle pulled the end of her scarf over her face, and sobbed into the wool, paying no heed to anything but the sound of her own distress.

She didn't notice the car stopping and the door opening right in front of her until, wiping the scarf across her face, she looked up. Sean's taxi had pulled up in the bus lane directly in front of her, and Sean was already lifting her suitcase into the boot.

'What are you doing?'

'Thought you could use a lift.'

Michelle opened her mouth to tell him she could manage perfectly well on her own, but stopped herself. Given that he'd found her at a bus stop, weeping like a Best Actress winner, he was probably justified in thinking she might need some assistance.

'I don't know where I'm going.'

As soon as she spoke the tears started up with renewed gusto.

'Woah!' She felt Sean's hand on her arm. 'Where do you live?'

'Leeds.'

'Right. Is there anyone you can stay with?'

Michelle shrugged, and swallowed, struggling to compose herself. 'I'm going to head home, I think.'

She saw Sean glance at his watch. 'Do you know what time your train's at?'

Another wave of tears started to well up behind her eyes. Michelle shook her head and took a deep breath. Enough crying already. Of course she didn't know what time the train was. She hadn't been planning on going home.

Sobs finally subsiding, Michelle realised that Sean's hand was still on her arm. Saying a silent prayer of thanks for the layers of jumper and duffle coat between his skin and hers, she pulled her arm away, and tried to adopt a more businesslike attitude. 'A lift towards King's Cross would be great. Thank you. I'm sure I can find a hotel if I've missed the last train.'

Sean stood next to the cab, holding the door. 'After you.'

He watched her climb into the car. She sank back into the seat and closed her eyes, shutting herself off, he couldn't help but feel, from any conversation with him.

He opened his mouth to say something and then stopped. The moment of indecision confused him. Usually people seemed to have no trouble opening up to him. And usually he had no trouble at all being charming. Sean had what his fifteen year-old nephew would call game. Maybe it was only situations requiring something more than an easy line that gave him a problem.

He turned to look out of the window, and watched the snow falling, hoping to summon the flutter of Christmas excitement back into his mind. Watching the fat flakes landing on the verges brought a smile to his lips.

'What are you smiling at?' Michelle interrupted his thoughts.

'The snow.'

'It's wet, cold and miserable.'

'It's fantastic. It changes everything.'

Michelle seemed to think for a

moment before answering. 'Jess said your family has a farm. I thought farmers hated bad weather.'

Sean shrugged. 'I'm not working today. Snow's great when you don't need to get anywhere.'

Michelle tsked at him. 'But we do need to get somewhere. You need to get to Edinburgh.'

'And you?'

'Back to Leeds, like I said.' There was a spark of irritation in her tone.

Sean paused. That feeling was there again in his gut. The same feeling that had made him stay at the airport with her. The same feeling that had made him stop his cab to pick her up. He told himself it was simply Christmas spirit. 'You're sure there isn't anywhere closer you could stay?'

'I could go to Jess's, but they only just got married. I don't want to intrude.'

Michelle turned away, apparently watching the snow falling outside the window, before turning back with a smile fixed in place. 'Besides I was always planning on spending Christmas on my own. It'll just be in Leeds rather than in the Caribbean.'

Sean grinned and matched her light tone. 'I'm sure you'll barely notice the difference.'

'Quite.' Michelle turned back to the window.

Sean let a silence fall between them. She'd asked to be taken to King's Cross to look for a train or hotel, so why hadn't he passed that request on to the driver? They were heading towards the apartment on the South Bank. As soon as he'd seen Michelle crying in the snow he'd abandoned the idea of catching the sleeper train to Scotland and decided to stay in London another night. But why? Because it was Christmas, and he felt bad about her being alone? That's what he was telling himself, but she patently didn't want his assistance. He thought about how she might react to arriving at the apartment. No matter how he played the scene out in his mind he couldn't see her taking it well. In the worst case scenario, he realised, it could be seen as a wee bit kidnappy.

'Michelle?'

'Yeah?'

'It's getting late.'

She nodded.

He took a deep breath. 'Look, I've been staying at a . . . ' He paused. ' . . . at a friend's flat. She's away. We could both crash there without paying for a hotel and then get a train in the morning?'

She shook her head. 'I'm fine, really. It's very kind, but . . . '

'But nothing. Why pay for a hotel when I'm offering you a spare room?'

'A spare room?' The hint of suspicion in her voice brought the grin back to Sean's lips.

He nodded. 'What did you think I was suggesting?'

She reddened. 'Nothing. I don't want to impose. A hotel will be fine.'

'What if I insist?' He could see the

indecision in her eyes, the wish to be independent, to not be reliant on anyone, competing with her tiredness and need to curl up and feel safe.

She sighed. 'You're sure it's no trouble?'

'None at all. In fact, it'll save me money, if the cab goes straight there.'

She shook her head. 'I'll pay for the cab, as a thank you.'

Sean wasn't really an insisting on paying sort of guy. He'd never felt emasculated by splitting a bill, and he could see that by paying for the cab, Michelle was able to tell herself that she wasn't relying on him. It made it a fair businesslike exchange rather than an act of charity.

'Ok.'

'Ok.'

She looked away from him again. Sean wasn't taking her acquiescence to imply that the drawbridge had been lowered for him to ride through. Why was he so interested in this woman? The almost kiss? That was certainly part of it, but that wasn't the beginning. He kept thinking of their first meeting before the wedding. She'd had spread-sheets and lists galore detailing every possible bridal need on the wedding day. It was obsessive. It was insane. It was a level of care for other people that touched something in Sean, something he'd started to believe might have been beyond repair.

' . . . the driver?'

He realised she was talking. 'Sorry?'

'What about the driver? You didn't tell him we've changed where we're going.'

Sean grinned in what he hoped was an innocent absent-minded sort of a way, and leaned forward. 'Straight to Ostler's Wharf, mate. On the South Bank.'

The driver shot a glance at Sean in the mirror but didn't comment. Sean rested back in his seat and raised an eyebrow at Michelle.

\* \* \*

The journey continued, off the motorway and into the city. Michelle focused her attention out of the window. The city was still bustling with shoppers, tourists and commuters rushing through the snow, hurrying to pick up last minute presents, or to get to the bar for Christmas drinks with friends. Everyone was moving like they had somewhere to be. Michelle realised that she had nowhere. She had a charitable offer of a place to stay from a virtual stranger, but nobody would be checking the clock and wondering when she'd be joining them.

The cab made it onto Westminster Bridge. The view down the river was stunning. The lights of the London Eye shone against the cloud-covered darkness, and the snow continued to fall around the wheel. You only needed the outline of a sleigh against the moon to make the perfect Christmas card. Michelle turned away.

★ ★ ★

A few minutes later she stood in the doorway of the flat and gasped. Firstly this wasn't a flat. Michelle lived in a flat. It had a bare patch in the carpet in front of the gas fire, and the spare room doubled as an airing cupboard. This place wasn't a flat; it wasn't even an apartment. This was a penthouse. The open plan kitchen-lounge-diner was bigger than her entire place in Leeds, but that wasn't what made her gasp. Sat right at the top of the building, the room was surrounded on three sides by glass, with views across the river to St Paul's Cathedral and the whole of the city beyond. Without thinking, she walked towards the window and stood for a moment, still and transfixed by the lights of the city spread out before her.

She heard Sean behind her carrying her bag into another room and then strolling back into the lounge.

'You like?'

'It's amazing.'

'I know. Shame it's not mine.'

'It must have cost the earth!' As soon

as the words were out of her mouth, Michelle apologised. 'Sorry. I just meant . . . your friend must be doing Ok.'

'Yeah.' Sean paused. 'Yeah. I guess she is.'

Michelle registered the 'she' without comment. Obviously, he could have female friends. That didn't mean that he was regularly and athletically bending them over the polished glass table. The thought caught Michelle by surprise. She must be tired, she decided. She clearly wasn't herself. She turned around to avoid Sean's eye and took a proper look at the rest of the apartment. It was elegantly furnished, but something seemed missing. 'Does she live here all the time?'

Sean nodded.

Michelle looked around again. There was a glass dining table surrounded by eight leather backed black chairs, a large L-shaped settee, a flat screen television and sound system mounted against one wall, and a gleaming gloss-black kitchen. 'Where's all her stuff?'

'What do you mean?'

'Well books, ornaments, DVDs, magazines. There's nothing here.'

Sean shrugged as if he'd never thought about it before. 'I don't know.'

She was being rude, commenting on his friend's home furnishing, which was not nice behaviour when he was letting her stay with him.

'There's a Christmas tree.' She gestured towards the modest tree in the corner of the room. It was the only personal touch she could see.

'I got that.'

Michelle was surprised. 'You're not even going to be here for Christmas!'

'You've got to have a Christmas tree.'

Michelle shook her head at the extravagance. She ought to be making herself useful. She glanced at the clock. It was nearly ten.

'Are you hungry?'

Sean nodded. 'I didn't get any dinner.'

'Well, that's not on. You've got to take care of yourself.'

The grin she was getting accustomed to spread across his face. 'I appreciate the concern for my well being.'

She met his eye. No obvious sarcasm. He was apparently sincere. Michelle looked away. 'It's silly not to eat.'

'Have you eaten?'

'That's not the point.'

Sean's grin widened. 'So let's eat.'

Michelle walked around the counter into the kitchen area and opened the massive American style fridge. 'There is nothing in here.'

'That's not true.' Sean walked up behind her and surveyed the fridge. 'There's eggs.'

He picked them up and peered at the box. 'And they're in date.'

Michelle turned and considered the options in the back of the fridge door. A small, slightly hard piece of cheese, an unopened bottle of wine and half a pint of milk.

'Right. Is there any bread?'

Sean shook his head.

'Well what else have you got?'

Sean looked around at the cupboards before flinging one open. It was full of plates. He furrowed his brow and tried the next cupboard along.

'How long have you been staying here?'

'Couple of weeks.' He shrugged. 'I eat out a lot.'

'Clearly.'

The picture in Michelle's mind was of Sean all suited up pouring wine in an elegant restaurant for an even more elegant woman. It wasn't great but it was an improvement on imagining what he might have got up to with the owner of this apartment. At least she could look him in the eye while she thought about him going out on dinner dates.

Sean's intrepid exploration of the cupboards revealed a sugar bowl, and half a bag of dried spaghetti. 'Pasta?'

'Is that all there is? Seriously?'

'Like I said, I eat out a lot.'

'Ok.' She took the bag of pasta and

popped it down on the counter along with the cheese, milk and eggs. 'Cheesy pasta then.'

'Sounds good.'

'Sounds like the only option.'

Michelle busied herself in the kitchen, finding that she seemed better able to work out where his mysterious lady friend stored the cooking essentials than he was.

Twenty minutes later she was spooning pasta into bowls and Sean was pouring wine into glasses. They sat opposite each other at one end of the dining table. Sean swirled a big mouthful of spaghetti onto his fork and tucked in. 'It's good. Cheesy.'

Michelle took a gulp of wine and allowed herself a smile. 'Considering the raw ingredients, it's practically miraculous.'

'You've worked wonders. Do you cook a lot?'

She nodded. 'It's a useful skill.'

'To make cheesy pasta?'

'To make something out of not very

much. Clever cooking is a great way to save cash.'

She took another sip of wine and Sean topped up her glass. She glanced at the goblet. She was drinking more quickly than she was used to.

'My mum taught me to cook.'

Why was she telling him that? The wine. It must be the wine.

'You're close to your mum?'

'I was. It was actually her idea that I take this trip of a lifetime holiday.'

Sean raised an eyebrow in question.

Michelle swallowed. 'It's what she wanted me to spend my inheritance on. She died. At the end of last year. Cancer.'

'I'm sorry.'

'It was very quick. She wasn't even ill really.' That still rocked Michelle. She'd had people close to her pass away before. Mum's sister, Auntie Barb, for one, but there'd been a progression: treatment; improvement; then more treatment; and a long interminable decline. There had been tasks Michelle could do; things that needed organising.

With her mum it had been different. A routine visit to her GP on Monday. Admitted to hospital on Tuesday. Officially dying by Wednesday. There had been conversations about hospices and specialist nurses, but there hadn't been enough time for any of those things. Tanya Jolly had been told by an official looking man in an official looking white coat that she didn't have much longer and her body had taken him at his word.

They fell silent. Normally Michelle would do anything to avoid talking about her mother, but tonight something felt different.

'People say I look like her.' She blurted the words out, pointing at her long red hair. 'I get this from her.'

'Lucky you.'

'Hardly. I sort of hate being ginger.'

'It's beautiful.'

Michelle wasn't sure how to respond. It was flattering, but she'd already let him get her back to this apartment and then drunk too much of his wine. Compliments were easy.

'What about your dad?'

Michelle shook her head. 'I don't really see him any more.'

Sean leaned towards her across the table and rested his hand on top of hers. 'I'm sorry . . . '

'I'm fine. They split up years ago.' She pulled her hand quickly away. 'I should clear these things away.'

'I can do it.'

'Right.' Michelle stopped half standing, half leaning over the table. 'I might go and er . . . could I take a shower?'

'Sure. Through the bedroom at the end of the hall.' He pointed to an archway beyond the lounge area.

Michelle strode down the hallway and found her case already sitting on the bed in the spare room. What was she doing, telling a virtual stranger about her personal life? This Christmas, she reminded herself, was about her independence.

The shower was excellent, not like the spluttery electric thing in her own flat. The water rushed over her body and numbed her sight and hearing, forcing her further into her own thoughts. She found herself back at her Auntie Barb's house, ensconced in the kitchen, as she and her mother generally were in the weeks after Dad's affair had been revealed. She remembered sitting on a high stool, with Dolly gripped tightly in her hand, watching her mother and her aunt making fairy cakes and biscuits, stews and pies, quiche — which Barbara insisted on calling flan — and sauces. She had seen how nothing was wasted. Tonight's leftovers were tomorrow's lunchtime soup.

Michelle stood under the shower, and relived all those moments. Time and time again she'd seen her mother proved right. Relying on other people left you in a mess. She'd seen clients who'd happily doled out cash to other halves who'd sworn blind they were going to use it to pay the council tax or the electric, and then been left alone, in debt and with threats of disconnection hanging over their heads. She'd seen countless friends through countless break-ups who all told the same story. They trusted him. They loved him. They thought he loved them. Michelle shook her head to clear her thoughts. Let other people make those mistakes. She'd been taught, by her mum, how to get along on her own.

And then she remembered watching Auntie Barb feeding the Christmas cake, pushing a skewer deep into the mixture and pouring a little brandy into each hole. Michelle paused on that memory for a second — revisiting the rich smell, and the sound of Auntie Barb's laughter when Michelle had poured far too much brandy. That must have been when she still thought they'd be going home to Daddy for Christmas. She remembered something else. Her mother standing in the corner of the kitchen, dabbing her eyes, refusing to join in with even the tiniest preparation for the festive season.

One final, more recent, memory snuck in uninvited. A single moment under a sprig of mistletoe. She stepped out of the shower, busying herself wrapping her hair and body in towels to distract from the unwelcome thought. She padded into the bedroom, to hear her phone buzzing in the pocket of her jeans. She fished it out. Jess's name was flashing on the screen. Maybe she'd changed her mind about having a best friend to stay for Christmas. With relief, Michelle swiped the screen to answer the call.

'Hi.'

'What am I going to do?' Jess's voice screeched down the phone.

Michelle pulled her towel tight around her and sat down on the bed. 'About what?'

'Patrick's present! It hasn't come yet.'

'Right.' Michelle didn't respond for a second before she forced herself to swallow her irritation. Jess needed her help, and helping each other out was what friends did. 'What were you getting him?'

She listened as Jess explained about the website, the perfect gift, and the unfortunately missed delivery man. Michelle made suggestions about contacting the warehouse, and failing that about making Patrick a 'voucher' for his perfect gift to open on Christmas Day. With her friend calmed, she relaxed a little; it was nice to have a few minutes to catch up with Jess after the excitement of the wedding. 'So are you excited about Christmas apart from that?'

'Yeah. Course we are.' Jess talked quickly. 'Thanks, Michelle. I'd better go.'

And she hung up. Michelle flicked her phone off and got dressed. Jess was bound to be preoccupied at the moment. They would have plenty of time to catch up in the New Year, she was sure.

★ ★ ★

Sean finished the washing up in silence. So Michelle had lost her mum. Was that what gave her the hint of vulnerability he kept seeing under the tough shell? Sean tried to picture his own life without the ever-growing gaggle of his family. Not possible. Family. Home. They were what made him who he was. They were what made Christmas what it was. They were what had kept him going when he thought he'd lost everything.

He dried his hands and turned the television on. There wasn't much to choose from with the time rapidly running towards midnight. He was still flicking between the channels when Michelle padded back into the room wearing a T-shirt and sarong tied around her waist.

She gestured towards the outfit. 'I packed for the Caribbean.'

'You look great.' He gestured towards the TV. 'This won't keep you awake, will it?'

She shook her head. 'Actually, I'm

not that tired. Eating late, you know, I think I've confused my body clock.'

'We could watch a movie?'

'Ok.' The idea of a film appealed to Michelle. She could imagine losing herself for a couple of hours, not having to think about her missed holiday, or about Sean, and definitely not having to think about Christmas. She squashed down into the corner of the L-shaped sofa, apparently trying to take up as little space as possible.

'Relax. Put your feet up. It's what it's designed for.'

Michelle stretched her legs out in front of her, causing her sarong to split apart revealing a long pale-skinned leg. Sean's eyes travelled up the leg and settled for a second on her thigh. He swallowed hard and turned back towards the television. 'Ok. Film. Wait there.'

Michelle watched Sean jog from the room and reappear with an armful of DVDs. 'Ok. I thought something festive would be in order. So *It's A Wonderful*

Life? White Christmas? Mary Poppins?
That one's not technically Christmassy
but near enough. The Santa Clause?
Elf?'

'Christmas films?' Her face was
incredulous. 'I'm assuming those came
with the apartment?'

'No! My mum buys me a new
Christmas movie every year. I own
them all. What do you fancy?'

'I'm not sure.' Michelle's heart sank.
She couldn't think of a worse way to
pass her time than being forced to sit
through a saccharine fantasy of Christmas. She was Sean's guest though, and
she had agreed to watch a film with
him. She sighed. 'Which is best?'

'You mean you haven't seen them?'

Michelle shook her head.

'None of them?'

'Mary Poppins, maybe, when I was a
kid.' Michelle swallowed the memory of
Christmas Eve, with her Dad, before
things changed. 'None of the others I
don't think.'

Sean was insistent. 'Then it has to be

a classic. *It's A Wonderful Life.*'

Sean put the DVD in the machine and leant back into the sofa clutching the remote. 'It's a bit cheesy but, you know, it's Christmas.'

Michelle watched the opening to the film in silence, uncomfortably aware that Sean was glancing at her to check her reactions. As time passed she lost herself in the story and forgot his attention. Sean had been right. The movie was pure cheese. As she watched George Bailey decide to end his life, Michelle rolled her eyes. She'd never had any time for self-pity. Life was tough and there was nothing to do but get on with things.

The film went on. The eye-rolling stopped. Michelle felt a lump rising in her throat, as George realised how many people in his life loved him. She swallowed it, and bit the inside of her cheek to distract herself.

As the credits rolled Michelle turned to see that Sean's eyes were streaming. He grinned at her. 'I love that film.'

Michelle looked away, giving him a chance to wipe his eyes. It was embarrassing, getting emotional in front of someone you hardly knew. Sean didn't seem to mind.

'I always cry like a baby though.' He grinned again. 'Very cathartic.'

'I don't really cry.'

'Erm, what about this afternoon?'

Yeah. He'd found her blubbing like a baby just a few hours earlier. She couldn't really argue with that. 'That was an aberration.'

'But didn't you feel better for it?'

Michelle thought for a second. Did she feel better? Well, possibly, but that was down to the meal, and the shower and the bed for the night. She felt better because her practical issues had been resolved. Sobbing on the pavement hadn't been any help at all. 'Don't be silly. Crying doesn't change anything, does it? It's far better to get on and deal with things.'

Sean shook his head at her. 'That's silly.'

The muscles in Michelle's jaw started to tense. How dare he call her silly? Silly was exactly what she wasn't. Silly was wasteful and irresponsible. Silly was childish. The Christmas tree twinkled in her peripheral vision. Christmas was silly. Michelle was not. She stood up from the sofa. 'I'm not silly.'

'You are if you think you can ignore your emotions. Feelings don't go away because it's inconvenient. Everybody has feelings they can't control.'

'Maybe not everyone.' Michelle paused. Maybe he was right. Maybe everyone else was a seething mass of love and hate and jealousy and compassion. Maybe there was something wrong with her.

'You've never had an emotion that overwhelmed you?' He stood up and moved towards her as he asked the question.

Caught off-guard her mind jumped back to the day when Auntie Barbara had unexpectedly collected her from school, and explained that Michelle and

Mummy would be staying at Barbara's house for a little while. Daddy, she had been told, would not be coming with them. 'Never.'

Another step towards her. 'What about your family? There must have been highs and lows.'

'Of course. Just not . . . ' She paused again. 'Just nothing worth dwelling on.'

'Fair enough.' Another step towards her. She could feel the warmth of his body radiating. 'What about passion? A boyfriend?'

'No one serious.'

He'd almost closed the gap between them now. Michelle wondered why she wasn't moving away, but she couldn't seem to make her feet shift. He reached one hand forward and touched her fingertips. The softest, most fleeting of touches, almost like a dream or a memory of a touch, and then he wrapped the arm, suddenly, decisively around her waist and clamped her body against his.

'You've never been completely caught

up in a moment of joy or passion? A moment where you couldn't think about anything else, where you have to do what you feel?'

Michelle shook her head mutely. Sean bent his head towards her. Involuntarily, she lifted her face to meet his. She could feel his breath on her cheek, his heart beating against her chest.

'You've never given in to a moment of desire?' He whispered the question against her skin.

'No.' Her answer was barely audible, muffled against his jaw.

His mouth hovered over her cheek.

'Fair enough.' He stepped away, releasing her from his arms. 'I guess we're all different.'

Michelle couldn't speak for a second. Her body was tingling from his closeness, and aching from the sudden distance between them. How dare he take advantage of her like that! A small voice in her head pointed out that firstly, no advantage taking had actually occurred, and, secondly, Michelle wouldn't have minded one bit if it had. Michelle ignored the voice.

'So you go with whatever you're feeling, do you?'

'Of course.' He glanced at his watch. 'Time for bed, do you think?'

His normal playful tone was back, which in this case, made the question sound even more like an invitation.

Michelle marched past him towards the spare bedroom. 'I'll see you in the morning.'

She undressed quickly and pulled the bedcovers around her like a cocoon. One more sleep, she told herself. One more sleep before you're back into your own flat, safe from all Sean's silliness. The only thing sillier than silliness, Michelle decided, would be falling for silliness.

\* \* \*

In the lounge, Sean switched on his laptop. While he waited for it to boot, he pulled his phone from his pocket, and flicked back to the message from Cora. Cora Strachan — he'd noticed a few weeks ago that she'd dropped the double-barrelled Strachan-Munro from her e-mail signature. He skimmed through the message again and sighed.

She'd stopped using his name, but she still kept texting. He'd sworn that they were over for good, but here he was staying in her apartment. He shook his head. Cora should be ancient history. He didn't keep slipping back into old habits because she was the love of his life. It was because it was easy. It was because it was safe.

He remembered finally quitting smoking two years ago. He'd spent five years trying. Patches, gum, hypnosis, cutting down gradually; he'd tried them all and nothing had worked. Then he'd stopped. No one-off sneaky smokes. No substitutes. He'd just stopped. Cold turkey. Maybe it really was the only way.

His laptop pinged into life and he

clicked his way to a train booking site, scrolled through the options for trains up the east coast the next morning and settled on the 11.41 from Kings Cross. As he clicked, an idea was forming that shoved any worries he had about Cora unceremoniously out of his mind. Maybe he could invite Michelle to spend Christmas with him? It would be in the spirit of Christmas, wouldn't it? An act of Christmas charity.

He glanced down the corridor, but the light in her room was already out. Best not to wake her. He clicked to select two tickets to Edinburgh, and paused for a second before clicking 'Confirm.' It would be fine, he told himself. Totally fine.

### Christmas Eve, 2013

Michelle was surprised to be woken by the sound of pots and pans crashing around in the kitchen. She pulled on the jeans and jumper she'd worn to the airport and headed into the lounge-diner in time to see Sean plating up the biggest cooked breakfast she'd ever seen. Bacon, sausage, fried eggs, fried bread, tomato, mushrooms and beans were being heaped vertically onto plates only designed for normal human-sized portions.

'There's enough here for about eight people!'

Sean nodded. 'Convenience stores don't really do single rashers of bacon. I had to buy a pack.'

'You've been shopping? What time is it?'

He glanced at his watch. 'Nearly ten.'

'Sorry. Oh God! Have I made you late for your train?'

'Not at all. I've booked us both on the 11.40. There's a cab coming at 11. Loads of time.'

'Right.' Michelle bristled at Sean's presumptuous attitude. 'I could have arranged my own train ticket, you know.'

'I don't doubt it, but I was booking mine.'

Michelle looked at the food and then at Sean. She remembered the state of the kitchen cupboards the night before. He'd clearly gone to a lot of effort to get breakfast ready. She must be sounding horribly ungrateful. 'Well, thank you. I'll pay you back for the ticket.'

He spread his palms in a 'no worries' gesture, and carried the heaped plates to the table.

Michelle sat down opposite him. 'Well this looks . . . ' She surveyed the mountain of food, unsure how to finish the sentence. 'This looks massive.'

Sean laughed. 'It's a long way to Edinburgh. Who knows when you'll get to eat again?'

'I'm going to Leeds.'

'Leeds. Edinburgh.' He chewed a forkful of beans and fried bread. 'Actually . . . '

Before Sean could explain, Michelle's phone buzzed in her pocket. 'Hold on.'

She got up from the table and

hovered in the kitchen to answer the phone. 'Hello.'

It was Jess again. 'They didn't have any pigs in blankets.'

'What?'

'The supermarket didn't have any pigs in blankets.'

Michelle laughed.

'It's not funny!' The pitch of Jess's voice escalated. 'I want it to be perfect.'

'It will be.' She felt for her friend. 'It's your first Christmas together. It won't be ruined because you don't have pigs in blankets.'

She heard Jess harrumph. 'That's what Patrick said.'

'Well then.'

They chatted for a few more minutes about how long roast potatoes took to cook, and whether you could still be viewed as a domestic goddess if you bought ready-made stuffing, before Jess hung up.

Sean had nearly finished his food mountain by the time she sat back down at the table.

'Sorry about that.' She waved her phone. 'Jess.'

Sean rolled his eyes. 'What's up with Princess Perfect?'

'What?'

'Jess.' He grinned. 'You've gotta admit, she's a bit spoilt.'

'Don't be rude.'

He laid down his fork and shrugged. 'Sorry. I know she's your mate.'

'Yes.' The comment had struck a nerve. She felt disloyal thinking it, but she wondered if Sean was right. 'She's a bit stressed about their first Christmas together. Wants it to be perfect.'

'Nah. Christmas isn't supposed to be perfect. It's supposed to be sort of disorganised. If you don't eat at least an hour later than you intended, you're probably not doing it right.'

Michelle didn't respond. She'd only eaten one proper Christmas dinner in the last twenty-years, and that one she'd prepared herself. It had been served precisely on schedule.

* * *

An hour later, they were on the concourse at Kings Cross station. Michelle let the noise and bustle wash over her, while Sean collected their tickets from the machine. All she had to do now was pay him for the ticket, make a polite excuse about being tired and preferring to sit on her own, and she'd be able to get back to her plan of spending Christmas alone as far away from tinsel or, indeed, mistletoe as possible.

She peered at the overhead display board. The 11.41 a.m. to Edinburgh, calling at Leeds, was on time. Her mood darkened, remembering that, by rights, she should be sunning herself in the Caribbean by now.

'Er . . . there's a little bit of a problem.'

She turned round to see Sean standing behind her, his rucksack slung over one shoulder and his hair flopping in front of his face. 'It's probably my fault, but . . .'

'What?'

'I think I must have clicked Edinburgh twice.' He held the ticket out to her.

'What?' She looked at the ticket. First class to Edinburgh. 'You did this on purpose.'

The words were out of her mouth before she had time to think about them, but as soon as she'd spoken she realised it was true. Sean was staring at the floor.

'Why?'

He took a breath. 'I'm sorry.'

She repeated the question. 'Why?'

'I was trying to be nice.' He paused. 'I should have asked you.'

Michelle didn't respond.

'Look, it's Christmas. It's horrible to be on your own. Why not come with me?'

'Because I barely know you.'

He stepped towards her. 'You could get to know me. I'm delightful.'

'You're a presumptuous little rich boy, who's too used to getting his own way.' Michelle took a breath. 'Write your address down and I'll send you the money for the ticket.'

Sean was disappointed and it showed on his face. 'It's reserved seating. I'm afraid we're next to each other.'

Michelle shook her head. 'I'll find somewhere else to sit.'

She picked up the handle of her suitcase, and set off wheeling her way through the throng towards the platform. There was no way she would be sitting next to that man. What on earth had he been thinking?

On the platform, she ignored the first class carriages and dragged her case down to the standard class part of the train. It was busy with people heading home for Christmas. Bodies, luggage and bags filled with presents were jammed into every available space. Michelle fought her way through, reading the reservations displayed above each seat, and discounting everything that started 'London to'. Eventually she found a single window seat which was only reserved from Newcastle onwards. She stripped off her coat and left it on the seat to stake her claim while she manoeuvred her suitcase onto the luggage rack.

Michelle sank into the seat and closed her eyes, but she couldn't relax. The carriage was filling up around her. Across the aisle was a mother with two young children and a bored looking teenage boy, who slumped into his seat and immediately started fiddling with his phone. In the aisle a group of older teenagers, students she guessed, were talking loudly and trying to make space to sit on the luggage rack.

'Finally!' The voice was female, the tone haughty, but with an undercurrent of thick West Yorkshire, which, Michelle guessed, the speaker had spent years trying to eradicate. The stranger gestured at the empty aisle seat next to Michelle. 'This is me.'

Michelle squashed tightly against the window to let the woman sit down and got a proper look at her companion as she did so. She was wearing a navy blue suit over a crisp white blouse, with dark court shoes. Her hair was cropped short and was unapologetically white. The outfit suggested conformity, but the hair said she didn't really care.

The woman eased herself into her seat and glanced at Michelle. 'Do you mind?'

She gestured towards her feet, which she was already easing out of the court shoes.

It seemed a little unusual, but Michelle smiled. 'Make yourself comfortable.'

As the train pulled away, and Michelle tried to concentrate on her novel, she realised the woman was staring at her.

'I know you.'

'I don't think so.' Michelle smiled and turned back to her book.

'I do. I don't forget a face.' The woman pursed her lips, as if her inability to remember was Michelle's fault. 'Turn your head that way.'

The instruction was delivered with

such certainty that Michelle obediently turned her face so the woman could observe her profile.

'I'll work it out. Where are you from?'

'Leeds.'

'Ah-ha! How old are you?'

'Twenty-nine.'

'Too old.'

'I'm sorry.' Michelle responded without thinking. The woman tutted. Again, Michelle felt as thought she was somehow at fault.

'Brothers or sisters?'

'Not really.'

'You're not sure?'

'Half-brothers. A lot younger than me.' Michelle petered off. Was the stranger expecting a full family tree?

Apparently not. She held up a hand. 'Don't tell me. It's coming!'

She screwed her face up in concentration. 'Joseph Jolly! And Noel Jolly. You're Noel Jolly's big sister.'

Michelle opened her mouth in surprise, but the woman stopped her again. 'I said don't tell me. Polly?

Molly? Holly! Holly Jolly! Two hundred new children to learn every year, and twice as many parents, but I never forget a face.'

'People call me Michelle.' Michelle peered at her companion. 'Mrs Bickersleigh?'

'Miss!' The tone was imperious.

'Sorry, Miss Bickersleigh.' Michelle heard herself chorusing the words like a schoolgirl, which was ridiculous. The woman had never been her teacher. So far as she could remember she'd only actually met her once, at Noel's nativity play. That must have been twelve years ago. Apparently, she truly never did forget a face.

'You can call me Jean. And, now I know this, you're Barbara Eccle's niece, aren't you?'

Michelle nodded.

'Barbara and I go way back. My brother took her to see The Beatles in Scarborough. 1963 it must have been. Waste of the price of a ticket that was. She wouldn't let him past her cardigan.'

The woman sighed. 'So what brought you down to London? Do you live here now?'

Michelle explained about the wedding, the cancelled flight, and the train ticket debacle. She skimmed over the mistletoe and the cheesy, weepy movie.

'You poor thing! You'll need a little something to perk you up after all that.' Jean produced a hip flask from her handbag, followed by two plastic cups. Michelle raised an eyebrow at the contents of the lady's handbag. Catching the look, Jean smiled.

'You never know when you might need a little pick-me-up. Chin! Chin!'

Michelle didn't even try to refuse. Drinking during the day wasn't her usual style, but she sensed that no argument would be brooked. She took a sip and felt the whisky burning her throat.

'That's the stuff. Now tell me about this boy.'

'Which boy?'

'The one whose house you slept at

last night. Why aren't you living it up in first class with him?'

Michelle took another sip of her whisky.

'Don't play with it girl. Drink up!' Jean topped up her cup. 'And tell me about the boy.'

'He's just a boy.'

'No. He's not. The ones people say are 'just a boy' are always something more.'

Michelle didn't answer immediately. She knew she was lying. Sean wasn't just a boy. He was all man. For all the floppy hair and mischievous attitude, there was nothing boyish about the way he'd pulled her into his arms. Outwardly, she shrugged.

'Nothing much to say.'

'Bollocks.'

Michelle gulped at the unexpected expletive, and looked again at her travelling companion. Jean rolled her eyes.

'Tell me about Noel then. Was it his mother I heard about a few months ago? Tanya Jolly? The one who died.'

Michelle shook her head. She really must stop drinking before talking to people. Her normal reserve had been shattered to pieces over the last twenty-four hours.

'Good.' Jean pulled a face. 'Horrid to lose one's mother too soon.'

'Actually that was my mother.'

'Oh. I see. I knew they were related somehow. Were you close to her?'

Michelle nodded. 'It was mainly just me and her when I was growing up.'

Michelle's plastic cup was topped up. She took another sip.

'So your parents split up? Your father married again?' Miss Bickersleigh was not, it appeared, a great respecter of personal boundaries.

'Yes. I didn't see him that often really.'

'That's a shame. Girls need fathers.'

The conversation was getting far too personal for Michelle's liking. She picked up her book and tried to look engrossed. Jean didn't seem to mind, but Michelle couldn't concentrate on the words. What was happening to her? Different faces swum across her imagination. Her dad. Sean. Auntie Barbara. Miss Bickersleigh. Sean. Her mum. Sean. Sean.

And then her dad again. A card every birthday. A letter every Christmas, always with an invitation to join him and Noel and Joe and The Elf. She'd never gone. She'd always said it was because of her mother, but why not this year? The letter had arrived a month before Christmas like it always did. She'd recognised the writing on the envelope and thrown it away.

And then Sean's face again. Those stupid green eyes glinting at her, challenging her to loosen up, relax, have fun. Those green eyes that clearly didn't understand anything about losing people that you loved, or about taking responsibility for yourself or anyone else. What Michelle needed wasn't Sean. It was simplicity, time on her own with no commitments. If she did happen to decide she wanted a relationship in the future, she would use one of those internet dating sites, where she could set criteria, and control who contacted her. It sounded much more orderly.

Finally, her mum. She would always think of her at this time of year, even though she'd hated Christmas with a passion. She remembered Christmas dinners after they'd moved out of Barbara's cramped terrace and into the flat — enchiladas, or homemade pizza, whatever Mum could think up that clashed with the season. She'd even written a cookbook based on the same idea — 'The Anti-Christmas Cook.' She wasn't exactly the new Delia but it had sold reasonably well, and given Tanya a career for the first time in her life.

Michelle's own book dropped onto her lap and her eyes settled closed, lulled by the rhythm of the moving train.

'Excuse me.' The voice seemed to be coming from outside. 'Excuse me!'

It was louder now, and closer.

'Excuse me!' Michelle opened her eyes, and looked around. She was still on the train, but Jean had gone. There was an empty seat beside her and a couple standing in the aisle. The man was glaring at her. 'These are our seats.'

Michelle rubbed her eyes and shook her head. 'No. This is only reserved from Newcastle.'

'Yes.' The man's tone was increasingly impatient.

'But we've only just left ... ' Michelle petered out as she looked around her. The family across the aisle had gone. The teenagers resting on the luggage rack had also vanished. She looked out of the window and saw unfamiliar buildings. She turned back to the couple. 'Where are we?'

'Leaving Newcastle, and these are our seats.'

'Right. Sorry.' Michelle swung her legs around and slipped past the man into the gangway. She hurried along the aisle, grabbed her case off the luggage rack and dragged it out of the packed carriage. She paused by the door and read the list of stations. Next stop: Edinburgh. Michelle groaned. Why hadn't someone woken her up?

Never mind. She'd have to get off at Edinburgh and then catch another train back to Leeds. Her immediate problem was finding somewhere to sit. Her hand went to the ticket, stuffed in her pocket. She had a reserved seat in first class. Of course, that would mean Sean. It was at least another hour to Edinburgh. She turned and peered back down the train, hoping desperately for a free seat.

\* \* \*

Sean stared out of the window as the train moved away from the built-up outskirts of Newcastle and on to cling to the coast towards Berwick. This part of the journey was always when he started to feel as though he was nearing home. Home for Christmas. He smiled to himself.

'Is this seat still free?'

He was jolted out of his reverie by the voice, but he didn't turn away from the window. After her reaction to him that morning, he wasn't minded to throw down the red carpet. 'I thought you were only going as far as Leeds.'

There was a pause. He glanced up at her.

'I fell asleep.'

Despite his resolution to be cool with Michelle, Sean's face cracked into a laugh. 'I guess you're stuck with me then.'

Michelle slumped into the seat beside Sean. 'Only until Edinburgh. I'm getting the first train back to Leeds.'

Sean paused. An idea, only half formed was jumping up and down in his head, demanding his full attention. 'What if . . .'

'What?'

'Look. I know we've only just met, but it's Christmas. It's silly to be on your own. Why don't you come with me?' The question surprised Sean almost as much as Michelle. He'd seen her reaction to the ticket to Edinburgh. At this point a sensible man would have known that it was time to give up, but he couldn't let go. He felt like his accelerator pedal had got stuck hard to the floor, and the only option was to hold on and enjoy the ride.

Michelle's lips pursed. 'We've been through this.'

'For goodness' sake. You're already halfway there. You'd really rather go back to an empty flat?'

Michelle's expression shifted slightly. He'd done enough sales pitches to see that she was interested, but she wasn't on the hook yet. Think Sean. What do you know about her? She's practical. Sensible. Somehow, he needed to make running away for Christmas with a virtual stranger sound sensible.

'Do you even have any food in your cupboards?'

Michelle shook her head.

'Right. Well, it's Christmas Eve now.

What are you planning on eating tomorrow?'

Michelle shrugged. 'Anything but turkey.'

Sean shifted in his seat to face her.

'We're not discussing this any more,' he tried.

No response. He was going to need to grovel at least a bit before he laid down the law. 'I'm sorry I bought the ticket to Edinburgh. It was out of order. I should have asked you first.'

'You should.'

There was a note of acceptance in her voice that hadn't been there before. Sean's stomach jumped. She might actually agree.

'Ok. What about a deal? It's Christmas Eve. What if you give me forty-eight hours? Two days. After that I'll drive you home myself. Forty-eight hours in the warm, with plentiful food and lots of Christmas spirit.'

'I'm not really a fan of Christmas.'

'Then I've got two days to change your mind. Deal?'

'Don't be silly.'

'It's not silly.' Two days. She might go for that, and it was only two days. Nobody could get their heart broken in two days. Sean grinned. This was it. This was his pitch. 'It's practical. It saves you wasting time and money travelling home. It saves you wasting more money at home on food and heat, and we both get some company.'

He held a hand out for her to shake, and waited. This was the sort of thing he used to do so naturally, follow his instincts because something felt right. Well, he'd done it now. No option but to stick with the idea and hope she didn't notice him trembling.

Eventually she took his hand. 'But only because it saves me a long trip home.'

Sean exhaled. 'Ok. Now for the terms and conditions.'

'What?'

'I'm a businessman. It's important that contracts are clear upfront. It saves all sorts of problems later.'

'But you can't add things now.'

'I'm clarifying our agreement. You have to enter into the spirit of things. No refusing to 'do Christmas'. No standoffishness. Basically you have to go along with whatever I say.'

'Whatever you say?'

'Absolutely. Forty-eight hours. I'm in charge.'

Michelle scowled. 'You're not in charge of me.'

'And you're pulling a face, which isn't very festive.'

'It won't make any difference. Christmas is for kids. We are not kids.'

Sean shook his head. 'What's wrong with being a kid at heart?'

Michelle didn't reply.

'So you agree to my terms?'

She nodded.

'Good.' Sean turned his face back to the window to give himself a moment to regroup. This was fine. It was only two days. Time limited. Just a bit of fun. He glanced back at Michelle settling back into the seat beside him, and felt his stomach lurch again.

# 4

Christmas Eve,
the previous year, 2012

## Michelle

'This is going to be great.' Jess is pouring champagne into two glasses.

'Isn't it a bit early for that?'

'Lighten up.' She shrugs. 'It's Christmas.'

'It's Christmas Eve, and it's half past nine in the morning.'

'It's exciting.' She carries her champagne into the living room and I follow her, leaving the second glass on the kitchen counter. 'Christmas with no family. It's going to be amazing.'

I ought to reply. I open my mouth but I can't make any words come out.

She claps her hand over her mouth. 'Oh my God! I'm sorry. I didn't mean 'no family' like . . . Sorry.'

'It's Ok.' She didn't mean anything by it, and it's been two months. Mum wouldn't be impressed if she thought I was moping. I force myself to smile.

Jess giggles. 'Is it wrong that I'm happy my parents have gone on a cruise over Christmas?'

I shake my head.

'So what about a cruise?'

'What?'

'With your money.'

'I don't think so.' I can't really see myself playing quoits with a party of retired librarians from Barnsley.

'Well you have to book something.'

I know I do. Mum was very clear about me spending the inheritance on a holiday. 'I don't even know how much it is.'

Jess's brow furrows again. 'I thought you saw to the solicitor yesterday.'

'Er . . . no.' I tried to go to the solicitors. I had an appointment. I got as far as the door. They had a Christmas tree in the reception. I could see it through the glass. It was a real one, like Dad used to bring home. I could remember the smell of the tree. I could remember Christmas with Mum and Dad still together. It wasn't the right thing to be thinking about. I'm supposed to be thinking about Mum. I didn't go in. I put a smile on for Jess. 'I'll phone them after Christmas.'

She takes another sip of champagne. 'So have you got everything we need?'

'What for?'

'For Christmas!'

I gesture towards her glass. 'Well we did have champagne.'

'You know what I mean. Turkey, little tiny sausages wrapped in bacon, Christmas pudding.'

'I don't like Christmas pudding.'

'Neither do I, but that's not the point. It's Christmassy.'

I close my eyes for a second. I was hoping for a quiet Christmas. 'Me and Mum never really bothered with Christmas food and stuff.'

Jess doesn't answer, but I can see her

nose start to wrinkle and a furrow appears between her eyebrows. 'I thought it would be nice, after everything.'

I'm being ungrateful. She's right of course. It will be nice to make an effort, and at least doing the traditional Christmas dinner will be different from all the years with Mum. 'Ok. What do we need?'

'Can we get a Christmas tree?'

I shake my head. 'No.'

I find a pen and paper and start to make a list. Jess, it turns out, has very firm ideas about what constitutes a proper Christmas. I put my foot down over the tree and insist that for two of us we only need a chicken rather than turkey, but apart from that it's Jess's perfect Christmas all the way.

The thought of braving the supermarket to get all this stuff on Christmas Eve doesn't appeal, but we can go together, and we've got all day. 'Do you want to drive to the shops?'

She wrinkles her nose again. 'Actually, I'm meeting Patrick for lunch.'

'Oh.'

'I mean, he's going down to London this evening, and I'm not going to see him until Boxing Day.'

Two whole days.

'You don't mind going to the shop, do you?'

'Course not.' Well someone has to go, and I'm not doing anything else, so I might as well make myself useful.

Jess skips off to make herself beautiful for the sainted Patrick. I collect my bag from the kitchen and get in the car. As soon as I sit down in the driver's seat I have one of the moments. I've never had anything like this before, but since Mum went they come every couple of days. It's not an upset feeling or anger or even anything you could recognise as grief. It's just the absolute certainty that everything in the world is just too vast and too empty and too pointless to contemplate. I sit in the car, staring straight ahead, and wait for it to pass.

## Christmas Eve, 2013

At Edinburgh station, Sean swung Michelle's case from the luggage rack and hopped from the train onto the platform. He set off towards Left Luggage and had checked in his rucksack and Michelle's suitcase before she had time to object. He strode out of the station towards the city.

'Aren't we going straight to your house?'

'Not yet. It's Christmas Eve. We're in the middle of the best city on the planet.'

Michelle opened her mouth.

'Don't argue. The best city on the planet, with a beautiful woman who says she doesn't like Christmas. This is part one of persuading you otherwise.'

Michelle made a face. 'It'll be really busy.'

Sean grinned. 'Full of potential new friends.'

'And cold . . . '

'Cold is Christmassy.' Sean leant

towards her, the now familiar scent of his skin filling Michelle's senses. 'We had an agreement. You said you'd go along with me for forty-eight hours. You're barely out of hour one.'

Pulling her duffle coat tight around her, Michelle followed Sean out into the city. There was snow on the ground, turning to slush as last-minute shoppers charged through it, rushing to get everything done in time for Christmas.

Michelle stopped as the cold air hit her. Sean paused alongside her, reached down, and took her gloved hand in his.

'What are you doing?' She pulled her hand away.

'Come on!' Sean leant towards her and retook her hand. 'You've got to hold hands on a first date.'

'This is not a — '

'Go along with it.'

'No.' Michelle stood still in the station entrance. 'I said I'd go along with Christmas. Holding hands is romantic not Christmassy.'

Sean sighed and let go of her hand.

'Ok. Come on then.'

Michelle was caught off guard as he strode away from the station and made his way over the bridge, away from the bustle of the Princes Street shops. She ran after him. 'Where are we going?'

'This way!'

She followed him along the road which twisted to climb steeply up the side of a long hill. Partway up, Sean turned and continued to climb up a narrow staircase between the buildings. Eventually they came out at the top of the hill and Sean settled leaning against a railing, looking out across the park and city in front of him.

'What have we come up here for?' Michelle came to a stop next to Sean, panting for breath after the steep, quick climb.

'Just look.' Sean placed his hands on her shoulders and gently turned her around to face the view.

The park below them was full of light and movement. She could make out the gleaming white of a skating rink, and a

Ferris wheel towering above the ant-like people on the ground. Next to the wheel there was a maze of tiny market stalls, all framed with sparkling lights. Beyond the market and the fairground, she could see trees across the park lit up with thousands of white lights, and beyond that Princes Street, still bustling in the last few hours of shopping time. It was only four o'clock but darkness had already descended, making the lights below sparkle even more brightly. Michelle gasped.

'You like?'

'It's very pretty.' The scene below her was like a piece of moving artwork.

'Excellent. Let's get down there then!'

Michelle sighed. 'It'll be really busy, and everything's always very overpriced at these sorts of things.'

Sean stopped dead in front of her. 'Forty-eight hours. You promised. Come on.'

And they were off again, racing back down the hill. Michelle had to skip and jog to keep up with Sean's irrepressible bounds, and was out of breath all over again by the time they got down into the market. She watched Sean weaving his way between the stalls, bumping into other shoppers, and shouting random apologies and excuse me's in every direction. Michelle followed more cautiously, squeezing herself between bodies, trying to blend in with the crowd.

And then she was alone. She looked around, and saw only strangers, unknown bodies jostling her, shopping bags bashing against her legs. She stood on tiptoes and craned her neck to see where he'd gone, but Sean had rushed too far ahead of her and was out of sight. She told herself to breathe. She forced her way through the crowd, and stopped at the end of a row of stalls. Behind her, a group of buskers were singing *God Rest You Merry Gentleman* but Michelle was deaf to their instructions to 'Let nothing you dismay.'

Sean had vanished. She was cold.

She'd been shoved and buffeted through the crowd from every direction. She hadn't had a chance to catch her breath from the run up and back down the hill. She was stuck in an unfamiliar city hundreds of miles away from home, and thousands of miles from the beach she was supposed to be lying on. And everywhere she looked there was bloody Christmas.

She walked a few metres in each direction, scanning the crowd. No Sean. She was absolutely, resolutely alone. She would have to go back to the station. Her case was there. Her only chance of getting back to Leeds was there. Of course she didn't have the ticket for the left luggage, and she had no idea whether she was too late to catch a train, but at the moment it was her only option. She stuffed her hands deep into her pockets and started to walk.

'Michelle!' At first the voice didn't seep into her brain.

'Michelle!'

'Hey! You in the red hat. Get that woman for me! Her! There! With the ginger hair!'

A hand touched Michelle's arm. 'Er, I think that man wants your attention.'

She turned to look where the stranger was pointing. Sean. Of course Sean. He appeared to be levitating above the crowd a few feet in front of her. He waved. 'I thought I'd lost you. Wait there!'

She watched as he clambered back down into the crowd, seeing that he had actually been standing on a high table in front of one of the glühwein stalls. He climbed down leaning on strangers, who seemed perfectly happy to assist, and lolloped through the throng to her side. 'Where did you go?'

'You were in front.' Michelle didn't smile. 'You went away from me.'

'I thought you were just behind me.' He beamed as a new thought entered his head. 'I told you it would be better if we held hands.'

Seeing that he was not, in any sense, forgiven, Sean changed track. 'Look. This was supposed to be about going with the flow. Trying to experience the joy of Christmas. You have to trust me.'

'I don't see how I can trust someone who runs off like a child the moment my back's turned.'

'I didn't run off. I went to see what was going on. You don't dive in.'

'Well, I'm sorry to be such a disappointment. If you give me the luggage ticket, I'll get my things and be on my way home.'

He could let her go. She'd probably still be able to get a train home. His brain was telling him to let her walk away. That would be safer. There was still a chance he wasn't in so deep that he couldn't swim back to shore.

He ran after her. 'Wait!'

He caught up within a few paces, and fell into step beside her. 'Now of course, you could go back to Leeds. You could. But, I can't help but wonder if that's really what you want.'

She shot him a look that left little doubt.

'Ok, so you do really want to do that, but I can't help but wonder if it's truly for the best. You're pissed off with me. I get that, although to be fair to me, if we'd held hands like I suggested we'd never have got separated.'

Another look.

'Anyway, you're here now. We're almost home, well my home anyway. There's a warm bed there.'

A further look.

'More than one warm bed. You'll be quite safe. Come on. If you go home now, you'll arrive back too late to go to the shops. You'll have no food in, and you won't be able to get anything until Boxing Day. It makes more sense to stay.'

'You think staying with you is sensible?'

Of course he didn't. Staying with him was clearly insane. 'Yeah. Dead sensible.'

Sean had played more than a few

hands of pub poker in his time, but those guys had nothing on Michelle. He had no idea which way she was going to jump.

'All right.'

'Really?'

She nodded.

'Come on then.' This time he grabbed hold of her hand and she made no attempt to wriggle free. He pulled her through the crowd to the foot of the Ferris wheel and into the queue.

Michelle pulled a face.

'What?'

'We've already seen the view for nothing from the top of the hill.'

'Well I'm going on it. You can stay down here if you want.'

Michelle looked up at the wheel turning slowly above their heads.

'No. I'll come on. I assume you're paying.'

Sean laughed. 'If it gets you to do something festive I'm more than happy to pay.'

They moved to the front of the queue

and climbed into a gondola, sitting opposite each other, knees touching in the middle of the car.

Sean's eyes never moved from Michelle. As the gondola climbed into the sky and paused at the top of the wheel, her whole face changed. The closed, guarded expression gave way to something else. Something joyful. She was smiling as she watched the people on the ground below. Finally, he seemed to have found something she liked.

The wheel turned them back to the ground and then they started to rise again. Michelle turned to face him.

'You're enjoying this?' He couldn't keep the hint of accusation out of his voice.

'Maybe. I haven't been on one of these things for years.'

'When was the last time?'

She shrugged. 'I don't know.'

'Liar.' The dig was friendly. 'Look, it's forty-eight hours and then you never have to see me again. What's to lose by telling me all your dark secrets?'

She laughed, quietly, tentatively. 'I don't know if I have any dark secrets.'

His responding laugh was generous and uncontrolled. 'Shame. Just tell me about the Ferris wheel then.'

'It was with my dad. We used to go to the fair near where we lived on Bonfire Night. We went every year, until they split up.'

'He didn't take you after that?'

'A couple of times. It wasn't the same. Mum would ask all these questions when I got home. And he used to bring The Elf with him.'

'The Elf?'

Michelle shook her head. 'Too long a story.'

'I wish I could say, 'Well it's a long ride,' but sadly it's not.'

They were coming towards the bottom of their third spin and the ride was slowing. Sean stepped off, and turned to help Michelle down, holding out his hand like a footman helping a grand lady from her carriage.

'What now?' Michelle was still smiling from the Ferris wheel.

'Food?' Sean suggested. 'And then I suppose we should probably head for home.'

'Ok. Where can we eat?'

Sean gestured towards a row of stalls. 'Hot pork rolls?'

Michelle nodded.

'And because it is Christmas, and the Ferris wheel was fun, but it's not technically Christmassy, you have to have glühwein.'

Michelle didn't argue, and they ate their rolls, crunching on crackling and giggling as the fat and apple sauce dripped onto their chins. The ride on the Ferris wheel and the comforting salty taste in her mouth were combining into a fun evening.

'Tell me something about you then.'

'Like what?' Sean glanced at her.

'I don't know.' She looked down at the floor, hoping he wouldn't see how awkward talking about herself still made her. 'I told you about my mum and the Bonfire Night thing. It's only fair.'

'Ok. What do you want to know?'

Michelle thought for a moment. 'Why do you love Christmas so much?'

She looked at his face while he thought about the question. His expression was almost wistful. 'It's because nothing can break Christmas. You can have the worst things happen one year, but then next year it's Christmas again and it's still exciting and brilliant. It's like Christmas is too special for real life to spoil it.'

'That's easy to say if you've never had a really bad Christmas.'

Sean shook his head. 'Oh, I've had lousy Christmases.'

'What happened?' Michelle didn't believe him for a second. If you had a really bad experience, you learnt from it. You learnt not to get your hopes up the next time.

'I once got dumped at Christmas.'

'Really? When?'

He waved his hand as if to dismiss

the memory. 'A long time ago.'

Michelle sensed that she'd reached the end of Sean's willingness to talk. She'd almost drained her glühwein, and opened her mouth to ask if Sean wanted another. She realised Sean wasn't drinking. 'You're not having any.'

'I have to drive.'

The information didn't make it through the glühwein fuzz in her brain until they were back at the railway station, collecting their bags. 'What do you mean drive? You said you lived in Edinburgh.'

'My flat's in Edinburgh. Christmas is at home.'

'Whose home?'

'Mine. Well technically, it's mine. Mum and Dad still live there.'

'Who's going to be there?'

'Just family.'

A full-on family Christmas? 'I can't come to Christmas with your whole family. I don't know them.'

'You know me.'

'Barely!'

Sean shrugged. 'Well you promised you'd do Christmas. Christmas means family I'm afraid.'

Michelle scowled, but knew that without anywhere else to go, she was well and truly beaten. 'Where is it then?'

He paused for a second. 'Near Edinburgh.'

He strode across the station to the car hire window and started talking and filling in papers for the assistant. Michelle watched in silence.

Once he'd collected the keys she followed him to the car park. 'How near Edinburgh?'

'Not too far.'

Something about his tone made her suspicious. 'How far exactly?'

'Couple of hours.' He looked at the snow starting to fall gently from the sky. 'Maybe three.'

He clicked the car key and opened the boot of the hire car. 'Would have preferred a four wheel drive in this weather to be honest.'

'What?'

'It'll be fine.' He glanced back at the snow. 'Probably.'

Without much other option, Michelle climbed into the car. It was clean and fresh, and had the recently valeted new car smell. She leant back into the passenger seat and settled to watch the scenery go by as Sean set off to drive out of the city. The radio was on, and a mix of cheesy Christmas music washed over them both. The snow falling had a hypnotic quality and the combination of the snowy cold outside and warm glühwein inside was cheering. She listened to the music, watched the snow, and resolved to try to follow through on her promise to embrace the Christmas mood. Life seemed to be giving her lemons. She would follow her mum's example, and do her best to make lemonade.

Her last conversation with her mother came into her head. 'Put yourself first, Michelle,' and then the instruction to use her inheritance for a holiday, a trip of a lifetime all for herself. She'd taken that as her mum's last lesson in independence, but what if she'd meant something else entirely? Put yourself first. Good advice, if you knew what yourself wanted.

Sean's voice interrupted her thoughts, as he swore quietly under his breath. They were well out of the city now, on winding narrow lanes. Sean switched off the engine. Why had they stopped?

'What's wrong?'

'Bit of snow.' He grinned over at her. 'Don't worry. Wait here a minute.'

He jumped out of the driver's seat and walked around the car. Straining in her seat, Michelle saw him stop and pull his phone from his pocket. After a minute he stuffed the phone back in his pocket and jogged back to the car. 'At least you're awake now.'

'I wasn't asleep.'

'You were drifting off before we left the station.'

'Oh.' That explained how quickly

they seemed to have got out of the city. 'What's the problem?'

Sean smiled sheepishly. 'Should have got a four wheel drive.'

He turned the key in the ignition and flicked the headlights on so she could see the narrow country road ahead more clearly. It was covered in a deepening layer of white.

'I told you snow was a pain. What are we going to do?'

'We'll be fine. We're nearly there. I've ordered us a taxi.'

'A taxi won't get through this!'

He laughed. 'This one will.'

'What do you mean?'

'Trust me.'

★　★　★

A few minutes later, Michelle heard a sound in the lane behind them. She spun her head. It was a tractor. 'That's never going to get past us.'

Sean had already jumped out of the car and was waving his arms in the middle of the road. He disappeared into the gloom. After a second, Michelle got out of the car to see Sean embracing an old man in a wax jacket that had probably seen its better days sometime before she'd been born. The man, apparently, went with the tractor, and, as soon as he released Sean from the hug, he was lifting bags out of the boot of the hire car and stowing them in the cab.

'Come on then.' Sean bounded back to her side of the car. 'Our lift's here.'

'What?'

'Oh. Sorry. Michelle, meet my dad. Dad, this is Michelle.'

The old man stepped forward. 'Alun.'

Alun turned to his son. 'Another one for dinner tomorrow then?'

Sean nodded, and Alun returned his gaze to Michelle. 'The more the merrier.'

Sean found a perch alongside his dad in the tractor, and leant down to take Michelle's hand, pulling her into the cramped cab.

'Not much space, I'm afraid.' He grinned and pulled Michelle onto his lap. 'Hold on.'

Michelle balanced herself on Sean's knee, her torso pressed against his body, his arm wrapped tightly around her waist to keep her in the cab. The journey couldn't have lasted more than twenty minutes but Michelle felt every second. Sean's breathing against her neck, his arm around her waist, his fingers inside her duffle coat gripping the fabric of her top to hold her steady on his lap. Heat raced through her body. Was he feeling it too? If he was there was no sign of it. He was chatting to his dad. Something to do with work and a farm she gleaned, but she struggled to concentrate on the conversation. She still didn't know what Sean did for a living. He seemed to be doing all right, if his willingness to buy first class train tickets for virtual strangers was any guide, but beyond that she had no idea, which made the heat in her body and the lightness in her head even more confusing. Relationships, in Michelle's world, were based on shared values and common interests, not on physical attraction, fairground rides and glühwein.

The tractor jolted over a bump, and Sean's arm braced to keep her secure on his lap. It was a long time since Michelle had spent this long this close to another human being. Her mum had never been one for big displays of affection, and Michelle had thought she was the same.

Another bump marked the entry to a farmyard. Through the dark and snow, Michelle could make out various outbuildings to one side of the yard, and a house to the other. The tractor pulled to a halt. Alun jumped down, and offered his hand to help Michelle out of the cab.

'You coming, son?'

'Sure.'

Alun dragged Michelle's case down from the cab and gestured towards the house.

'Right in there. Sean'll show you what's what.'

And he headed off.

Michelle glanced at her watch. After midnight. She turned back towards the tractor. 'Are you Ok?'

Sean grinned and stretched to uncurve his cramped spine. 'Fine. Let's go in.'

He jumped from the cab and grabbed hold of her case. 'Don't mind my dad. Man of few words. You'll understand when you meet Mum.'

Michelle followed Sean towards the house and into the darkened hallway. The ceiling was low and the stairway was narrow. She got the impression of an old cottage, which had probably been extended and remodelled by generations of occupants. Sean leant past her to shut the door, moving his body in close to hers. A hush fell over them. She could hear his breath, and feel the warmth from his body. She raised her face to meet his lips. The kiss was softer than she expected, and more lingering. Without thinking about it, she parted her lips and reached her hand to his waist. Sean raised his fingers to her cheek, and traced her jawline, sending a flush of warmth through her body. The world beyond the tiny dark hallway faded away.

Sean pulled back.

'Sorry.' He turned his head away from her face. 'That was out of order.'

'It's Ok.' She mumbled the words into her chest.

'Yeah.' He tried to arrange a smile on his face. 'Just got a bit carried away. Christmas spirit and all that.'

He took a big step back from her. 'Right. Wait here. I'll go find you some towels and work out who's sleeping where.'

He disappeared up the staircase at the end of the hallway. Michelle leant back against the wall. Her heart was beating hard and fast. Stupid, stupid, Michelle. Clearly Sean had instantly regretted what had just happened. He had just been being friendly. Nothing more.

Sean jogged back down the stairs, arms now full of towels and bedding, and stopped a clear two metres out of touching range. 'It's a bit of a full house.'

'Who's here?' Michelle remembered that she wasn't just spending Christmas with a man she barely knew; she was spending it with his whole family.

Sean waved a vague hand towards the upstairs. 'Oh, people.'

He pushed one of the doors off the hallway open. 'Brilliant. No one down here.'

He turned back to Michelle. 'I'm sorry. Are you all right on the sofa?'

She nodded.

'Good.' Sean busied himself spreading sheets, blankets and pillows over the sofa.

'There's a shower room down here too, through the kitchen.' He pointed towards another doorway, and flung a towel over the arm of the settee. 'So are you sure you're Ok there?'

Michelle nodded again. 'Where will you be?'

Sean shrugged. 'On a floor some-where by the looks of things.'

'You could . . . ' Michelle stopped herself. She'd already made a fool of herself with the kiss. She wasn't going to get rejected again.

'What?'

'Nothing. I'll see you in the morning.' Michelle nodded brightly.

'Right. Goodnight then.'

Michelle sat on her makeshift bed and listened to Sean's footsteps disappear upstairs. She found the rumoured shower room and brushed her teeth. Back in the lounge, she snuggled down into the surprisingly comfortable cocoon he'd built for her, and tried to think about anything other than that kiss.

\* \* \*

Upstairs, Sean tried to settle on the floor of his sister's childhood bedroom, which was already occupied by his brother, Luke, in the bed, and fifteen-year-old nephew on the foldout bed. A quick survey had told him that it was the least occupied room in the house, as his sister-in-law and the baby were packed into the old nursery, and his sister, her husband and the twins were all but stacked vertically in his and Luke's old room. A full house for Christmas — just how his mum liked it.

The floor was hard and he'd been left with the oldest, least presentable of the available bedding, but it wasn't discomfort that was keeping him awake. Normally he could sleep anywhere without a problem. What had he done? He'd brought a girl he hardly knew all this way on an impulse. His thoughts turned back to the last time he'd acted on impulse in a relationship. Cora. Perfect, particular Cora. The promise to build a life together. For better or worse and all that. Promises made on impulse, Sean knew, were easily broken, and the hearts that made promises were collateral damage at best.

Broken promises. Broken hearts. Both those things were hard to mend.

Sean's thoughts raced between two extremes. He was dismayed with himself for bringing Michelle here, for kissing her, for stopping kissing her, but, at the same time, the Christmas Eve feeling was growing in his gut. The feeling of anticipation, the childlike wondering about what tomorrow might bring. It wasn't a feeling he was used to any more, but somewhere in the back of his mind he knew exactly what the feeling was. One more sleep, he thought.

# 5

## Boxing Day, 2002

### Sean

It's six o'clock in the morning. I'm wide awake. Nobody should be awake at six o'clock in the morning on Boxing Day. Boxing Day is the ultimate lie-in day. There's nothing to get out of bed for on Boxing Day.

That's bollocks, of course. We live on a farm. My dad got up hours ago. I should get out of bed and do some work, but I don't. I lie and stare into the darkness and wait for Cora to be awake too.

It's too dark to see, but I know the pile of paper is still sitting on the chair at her side of the bed. The prospectus. The acceptance letter for the course starting in January. The application form, two-thirds completed in my wife's best writing, for single person's accommodation.

Really, this is my fault. I was pissing about last night, asking where she'd hidden my Christmas present. I said it didn't matter if she told me now, because Christmas was over, and then I started pretending to look in places that it might have been. She told me to behave like a grown-up. She tells me that a lot lately. I pulled this shoebox down from the top of the wardrobe and she went mental.

I opened the box. I shouldn't have opened the box. If I hadn't opened the box I wouldn't have found all that stuff, and I wouldn't know. If I didn't know it would still be like this wasn't happening. I wouldn't be lying awake on Boxing Day morning waiting for my wife to wake up so we can chat, like the grown-ups she wants us to be, about precisely how and when she's planning to leave me.

# Christmas Morning, 2013

## *Michelle*

'What is she?'

What was happening?

'She's a lady.'

Two voices wrenched Michelle from sleep.

'I know that. What is she doing here?'

She opened one eye. A girl, in pink pyjamas, clutching a teddy bear.

'Maybe Santa brought her.'

Michelle opened the other eye. A matching boy, blond curls sticking every which way, tiny glasses perched on his button nose, clinging to his sister's arm.

'I think she's awake.'

The girl extended a hand towards Michelle. 'Good morning, lady. My name is Chloe Patterson. Did Santa bring you?'

Michelle freed one arm from the blanket and shook hands with Chloe Patterson. 'No. I'm Michelle. I'm

Sean's . . . ' She searched for a word. ' . . . friend.'

The girl nodded. 'Like Amy McAvoy. She is my friend.'

Michelle smiled. 'Yeah. Like Amy McAvoy.'

She turned to the boy and extended her hand. 'And you are?'

The boy peered at Michelle uncertainly, and let his sister carry on the talking. 'He's Joseph. You can call him Joe or Joseph, but not Joey because it makes Mummy cross. He is shy.'

'Very good.' She thought for a second of her own half-brother, Joseph. What was his family Christmas like? Michelle focused her smile on the Joe in front of her. 'Nothing wrong with being shy.'

'Mummy said we could pick one present from under the tree to open with breakfast.' Chloe pointed towards the Christmas tree in the corner of the lounge.

In the beginnings of the morning light, Michelle considered the tree properly for the first time. It was beautiful. Thick, dark, green needles. Tall and full at the base. She swallowed. 'It's a lovely tree.'

Chloe nodded. 'It's one of Uncle Sean's. He always gets Nana and Granddad the best tree.'

One of Uncle Sean's? Who has more than one Christmas tree? Michelle put the thought aside as a misunderstanding of a little girl. The children had lost interest in her and were happily pulling presents from under the tree. Sitting up on the sofa, Michelle listened. She could hear people moving around in other parts of the house. So this was it. Christmas morning in a family home. She took a deep breath.

'What are you two doing?' An older woman bustled into the lounge, wearing a pinny over her dressing gown.

'Mummy said it was all right.'

The woman sighed. 'Oh, did she now?'

Her attention finally alighted on Michelle. 'Oh, hello my dear. You must be Sean's friend. Alun told me he'd brought someone back. I can't tell you how pleased I am. It's been so long since he brought anyone home. I was starting to think that it would never happen, or that he'd started batting for the other team. Not that I'd have minded that of course. Alun might have had a cow, but I'd have said to him, 'Alun it's the twenty-first century. These things are all the rage these days.' So I wondered if that was it. I thought maybe he was shy about telling his Ma. Cameron MacGregor was like that, you know. He didn't say a thing. Of course his mother had known for years. She heard it from someone in her knitting circle, as it goes. But anyway, here you are. All woman.'

Michelle wasn't sure how to respond. She hoiked the blanket up a bit higher over her boobs.

'You'll be wanting some breakfast. I'm sorry I didn't have anything for you last night. If I'd known he was bringing someone I'd have left something out. There's a bit of ham needs using. You could have had a sandwich. Or egg. We've always got eggs. Do you like egg?'

Michelle nodded.

'Well, everyone does. You rarely meet a person who doesn't like egg. Mind you, I was at school with a girl who wouldn't eat the whites. Yolks, not a problem, but never the white. Made scrambled egg a right performance.'

'Chloe!' A new voice shouted from the hallway before coming into the room. Another woman, maybe a couple of years younger than Michelle. 'Oh! Hello.'

The older woman continued. 'This is Sean's friend. Isn't it wonderful? Can you remember the last time he brought someone home? I was telling her how we were starting to wonder . . . '

The younger woman cut in. 'Hi. I'm Bel. Isobel. People call me Bel.'

'Michelle.'

'I'm Sean's sister. Do you want some breakfast?'

Michelle nodded, noticing that the

older woman was still chatting away quite happily, oblivious to the fact that her audience was moving on. She followed Bel into a kitchen-dining room, where the other woman poured herself a generous cup of coffee and an equally generous Buck's Fizz. Michelle gladly accepted the offer of the former, declined the latter, and sat down at the massive wooden table.

'Don't mind Mum going on about Sean.'

Michelle smiled. 'I won't. We really are just friends.'

The other woman smirked. 'Course you are.'

'We are.' Michelle could feel her cheeks colouring. 'I actually only met him two days ago.'

'Woah!' Bel pulled out the seat opposite Michelle and sat down. Her face opened up into a big wide toothy smile with echoes of Sean's own familiar grin. 'Talk about acting on impulse. He must have got it bad.'

'No!' Michelle shook her head. 'It's

not like that. I got stranded in the snow. I think he took pity on me.'

Because that was all it was, Michelle told herself. The kiss last night had clearly meant nothing to him. It was an aberration, best forgotten.

'If you say so. Really don't mind Mum. I don't know why she got it into her head that he might play for the other team. I mean, he got married for goodness' sake!'

Married? Michelle swallowed hard, pushing down the bile that was rising in her throat. Married. Well, that was that then. Any interest he might have had in her was nothing more than a mouse playing while its cat was away.

'Oh my God!' Bel clamped her hand over her mouth. 'You knew that didn't you? I haven't massively ballsed things up, have I?'

Michelle shook her head and tried to make her lips into a smile. They didn't seem to remember where to go. 'We really are just friends.'

'Thank God! Seriously, I'm getting

worse than Mum with my mouth. Don't know when to stop talking. That's my trouble.'

Michelle made another attempt at a reassuring smile, but she wasn't sure how convincing her unconcerned act was. She wasn't that convinced by it herself.

The tension eased as the room filled up and Michelle was introduced by Bel to her husband, her other brother, Luke, and his wife and children. She had a cuddle with the baby, and busied herself with introductions and chit-chat and anything that wasn't thinking about Sean. She was almost managing it, when the man himself surfaced and poured himself an even bigger mug of coffee than his sister.

She watched him lean against the kitchen worktop sipping his coffee. Married. He got married. That's what Bel had said, not that he was married now. Michelle felt her stomach flip. It might only have lasted a few weeks. It might have been a quickie wedding of convenience to get some poor Ukrainian farm worker a visa. His wife could have left him years ago, or he left her, or she died. Michelle's hopes rose with the thought, and then she felt guilty for wishing this stranger dead. Her stomach flipped again. Bel hadn't said that he wasn't married now either though. Michelle forced herself to take a deep breath. It was irrelevant. She didn't care for him either way.

\* \* \*

After breakfast, Sean watched his family bustle Michelle away into the lounge. He hung back, unexpectedly uncertain how to approach her. Should he pretend the kiss hadn't happened? Go back to their nice safe agreement, that this was forty-eight hours of Christmas cheer and then back to their normal lives?

Sean's father was sitting alone at the table. 'What are you doing?'

Alun raised a finger to his lips and

160

then pointed at the open door behind Sean. He closed the door and sat down at the table.

'Getting some quiet. It's a mad house through there.'

Sean laughed. 'Always is in this place.'

Sean's phone beeped in his pocket. He scrolled quickly through the text, hit delete and switched the phone to silent.

His father raised an eyebrow in question.

'Cora.'

'Ah, and what does the former Mrs Munro want this fine morning?'

'This and that.'

'And I trust she'll not be getting either of them from you any more?'

Sean shook his head.

'Probably best.'

'What am I going to do?'

'About what?'

Sean didn't answer.

'Let me guess. About the fine young red-headed lassie you managed to bring home?'

Sean nodded.

'You like her?'

Sean paused. He nodded again.

'I should imagine the best thing would be to just go for it. You don't get anywhere in life sitting on the sidelines.'

Sean shook his head. 'Not this time.'

'Ah, you're not still on Cora.'

Cora. The last time Sean had dived right into a relationship, and it hadn't worked. He had to rebuild his whole idea of who he was and what love was, and it didn't involve diving straight in any more. 'Well look where I ended up.'

'You ended up here.' Alun sighed. 'Look. I don't do so well with talking. I leave that for your mother.'

'She doesn't give you much choice.'

'Watch what you're saying about your mother.'

Sean's head dipped. 'Sorry.'

'I should think so. Anyway, you jump in if that's what you want to do. Since Cora you've been cautious when it comes to the girls. It's not you. You're a jumping in with both feet man.'

'I don't know.'

'I do. Look at this place. I retired five years ago. You increased the business more in your first year than I did in the last twenty-five, by just going for it. I was terrified the whole time. Thought you were going to lose me my house, but no. You went for it and it paid off.'

'I'm scared.'

Alun grunted. 'Well that's no good reason not to do anything now, is it?'

Could it be that easy? Could he really step up to the edge of the cliff and jump with no idea at all whether she'd catch him? No safety net of telling himself he'd never see her again. No pretence that this was forty-eight hours of madness and then he could walk away. Could he?

'I don't know.'

His father shook his head. 'Well you'd best make your mind up. I just don't reckon you can change who you are. Not doing something because you're scared. It's not you.'

Sean pushed his chair back from the table and stood up. 'Right then.'

★ ★ ★

Michelle spent the morning discovering that one of the joys of a big boisterous family, desperate to include her in all their activities, was that it made it surprisingly easy to avoid one specific member of that family. She went upstairs with Bel to find some clothes to borrow. She admired the twins' new toys, and allowed them to pull her into an elaborate game of dolls versus dinosaurs, a pastime that appeared to be well-established as their joint favourite. She won grudging kudos from Sean's teenage nephew by working out how to get music to download onto his brand new Christmas present smartphone. She won grudging respect from Alun with her ability to chat about savings rates and pensions options. She offered to help Sean's mum prepare dinner, and was decisively bustled out

164

of the kitchen. And that was her mistake, because that left her in the hallway alone and unchaperoned.

'Get your coat.' Sean was leaning on the wall next to the front door.

'Why?'

'I want to show you something.'

Sean watched Michelle as she looked down at the skirting board, rather than at him. So he hadn't been imagining it earlier. She was avoiding him. He'd blown it with that kiss. 'Look if it's last night, I'm really sorry. I was out of order. It won't happen again.'

His eyes flicked to the floor as he spoke, evading her gaze. He shouldn't be promising that. It was pretty much the opposite of what he should be saying.

She blinked hard. 'Fine.'

'So you'll let me show you?'

She nodded, a small curt nod. He grabbed both their coats from the hook in the hall before she could change her mind. Then he stopped in the doorway. 'Wait. What shoe size are you?'

'Six or seven. Why?'

He scrabbled on the floor in the porch and came up with two wellingtons. 'Don't want your shoes getting messed up.'

'Where are we going?'

'Just outside, but you are on a farm. Remember?'

Michelle kicked off her shoes and pulled the boots on. 'These aren't a pair.'

'Do they both fit?'

'Sort of.' She glanced at his face. 'Probably good enough.'

Sean grinned. 'All right then. Come on.'

He bounded out into the farmyard, noticing that the hire car they'd abandoned last night was parked next to the small barn. His dad must have gone out at first light to collect it. He carried on across the yard. He really did want to show her this. It had been in his mind since he very first suggested the whole 'forty-eight hours of Christmas' plan. He glanced at the sky. It was clear and blue, and last night's snow was crisp and untrodden on the ground. Perfect. He led the way across the farmyard and between the two biggest outbuildings to a padlocked gate which he climbed over.

'Are we allowed through here?' Michelle had stopped at the gate.

'Course. It's my land.' Sean walked back to the gate and held out his hand to help Michelle climb over. She didn't take it, managing to get over on her own.

'Well your parents' land.'

'No. Mine.' He carried on along the track beyond the gate before turning to climb a second gate on the right into a field. Again, Michelle refused his help.

He stopped at the edge of the field. 'Look.'

'Wow!'

She couldn't stop the exclamation escaping her lips. Even for a Christmas non-believer, the sight in front of her was breathtaking. Stretched out across the field was row upon row of miniature

Christmas trees, waist high, all covered in a dusting of white snow.

'These are for next year.'

'You farm Christmas trees?'

Sean nodded, smiling broadly. 'Dad started it as a sort of sideline to the farm. Locals could come and pick their own tree. When I took over I turned the whole thing over to trees.'

'Seriously? You make Christmas trees?'

'Grow Christmas trees.'

Michelle pulled a face. 'You know what I mean.'

Sean nodded. 'We've got a bigger growing site over by Loch Lomond. Most of these we still sell locally. The main site's for trade, garden centres, local councils, hotels, that kind of thing.'

'So you actually make your living out of Christmas?'

'I own another nursery, and a tenanted farm the other side of Edinburgh. Not good business to have all your eggs in one basket, but yeah. Christmas trees are my main thing.'

'But you still love it?'

Sean looked confused. 'Wouldn't do it if I didn't love it.'

'Don't you get sick of all the Christmas?'

Sean shook his head. 'Never. Why do you hate Christmas so much?'

She shrugged. It wasn't a question she wanted to answer. It was a joke amongst her friends and colleagues — the idea that she was a bit of a Scrooge. She went along with the jokes to avoid anyone asking her the question too seriously.

'What was Christmas like when you were a kid?'

She kept her eyes fixed forwards, looking out towards the field. 'Depends when you mean exactly.'

'What do you mean?'

'My dad was insane about Christmas. Always made a massive deal of it. He was Santa for this big department store every year. Properly obsessed with Christmas.'

'Cool.'

'Maybe.' Michelle paused. She didn't usually talk about her dad, but this felt different. She was far away from home, and Sean was easy somehow. Even with all the question marks in her head, when she was alone with him things felt safe. And anyway, she'd promised him forty-eight hours. What did it matter what you said to somebody you were never going to see again?

'I remember sitting on my dad's knee when he was all dressed up as Santa. I knew it was him, but it didn't matter. It felt like magic.'

Sean nodded. 'That's the point of Christmas. You can know it's all tinsel and costumes and a dead tree, and still love the magic.'

'Maybe.'

'So what about the other times?'

'What?'

'You said Christmas depended on when it was.'

Michelle nodded. 'I told you about their break up, Mum and Dad. Mum kind of avoided Christmas after that.'

Thinking of her mum, Michelle suddenly felt disloyal. Her mum had been there for her right through the year. Christmas was just one day.

'And she was right. Do you know how much the average adult spends on Christmas every year?'

Sean shook his head.

'I do. £592. That's nearly £29billion across the country. It's insane.'

'But it's not about the money. It's about family and getting together and that feeling of . . . ' Sean dried up for a second. 'That feeling of anticipation, of hope. Don't pretend you don't understand that.'

'It's a commercialised excuse to overspend. Anyway, it's for kids really, isn't it?'

Sean wasn't having that. 'I saw your face.'

'When?'

'When you saw all this, the trees and the snow, and when you were talking about your dad and the magic.'

'This is quite pretty.'

'It's not just pretty. It's Christmas. We're standing in a field, in the freezing cold, and you gasped because it's Christmas.'

'Maybe.'

'Do you still talk to your dad?'

Michelle shook her head. 'He's got my number. He texted to say Merry Christmas.'

'You should ring him.'

Another shake of the head.

'Why not?'

'Too much water under the bridge.' Christmas or not, she didn't want to play at happy families.

'When did you last talk to him?'

She shrugged. 'I e-mailed him when Mum died. I thought he ought to know.'

'Did he come to the funeral?'

'I didn't invite him.'

'Ok. Look, it's Christmas. It's about family. A two minute call couldn't hurt.'

'I don't have signal.'

'No excuses. Does he Skype?'

'I don't know.' She paused, realising

172

that Sean wasn't going to let this drop, and that she didn't want him to let it drop. It was an odd feeling. Someone else was taking care of her. That was what Sean was doing. Picking her up at the airport, taking her to the Christmas fair, getting her to talk about her family — they were all the acts of a man who was thinking about what might be best for her. She pulled her phone from her pocket.

'I thought you didn't have signal.'

She scrolled back through her phone and found the message she was looking for. 'He sent me his Skype name though.'

'Come on then.'

Ten minutes later she was sitting in front of the computer in Sean's office, downstairs in a newer extension to the family home.

'I'm not sure about this.'

Sean shrugged. 'It's two minutes out of your life.'

'He's probably not even online.'

He was online.

Michelle waited as the image came up on the screen, and Sean adjusted the speakers so she could hear properly.

'Holly!' Her father was, as always, in his Santa costume. If he was surprised to hear from her after such a long time, it was hard to tell under the thick white beard and the Father Christmas hat, but she saw him turn and gesture to someone out of sight of the camera. 'It's Holly!'

He turned back to face the screen. 'Ho! Ho! Ho!'

'Hi, Dad.'

In the background she could see other figures moving around, her half-brothers, tall gangling teenagers now, not the snotty kids she remembered.

Behind her she heard Sean stifling a chuckle.

The image on the screen was of Santa's grotto packed into a terraced house in Bradford. There were lights, dancing Santas, illuminated reindeer, inflatable snowmen, tinsel, so much tinsel, all jammed into the tiny living room. Another figure came into the shot.

'Holly!' The woman was clearly in her late forties, but dressed, apparently without embarrassment, as an elf. The Elf. 'Happy Christmas!'

'Happy Christmas, Sandra.' Michelle forced the words out through clenched lips.

Her father took over the conversation, eagerly telling her about their family Christmas. Michelle listened.

Her father paused. 'You know you're always very welcome here, don't you?'

Michelle nodded. He'd always been clear about that. He'd never tried to make her pick sides, but that is what she'd done. She'd chosen to be Tanya's daughter.

'And your mother, I didn't know if you'd want me to come . . . ' He looked away. 'I am sorry.'

'Yeah.' It was all Michelle dared say.

'Good.' He looked smaller somehow.

175

Michelle pushed a smile onto her face. 'Well I'd better get on. I just wanted to say Merry Christmas.'

'Thank you, pet. I appreciate it. I do.' He paused. 'Maybe in the New Year you could come for a visit?'

She gave a tiny nod. It wasn't much, but it was something, and that was more than they'd had before. Michelle could feel herself starting to tear up. She took a breath.

'Ok. Better get going.' She clicked the disconnect button quickly before Sean saw her get any mushier.

'Woah.' She was still staring at the screen when the voice behind her cut in.

'What?'

'They really go for it with the Christmas decorations.'

'You don't know the half of it.'

Sean swung himself onto the desk in front of her. 'Tell me.'

Michelle turned to face him. There didn't seem much point lying about it now.

'The decorations aren't because it's Christmas.'

'What?'

'He has it like that all the time.'

Sean's face convulsed as he tried not to snigger, turning redder and redder until his eyes watered, and he gave up under the pressure. A gale of laughter shook his whole body. 'You're kidding?'

She shook her head. 'He wasn't as bad when I was little, but after they split up it got more and more and more.'

'Wow! That must have been brilliant when you were a kid. Christmas all the time!'

'It was mortifying. I could never take a friend there. And my mum hated it.'

'Fair enough, but you're not your mum.' Sean stepped towards her. 'I mean, it's bonkers, but it is kind of fun.'

'I guess.'

'Do you know why they split up?'

Michelle nodded. 'He had an affair with the elf.'

Another torrent of laughter. 'I'm sorry.'

'Well, men have affairs with their secretaries all the time. His job was being Santa, so he had an affair with his elf.'

'Right.'

Michelle sighed. 'I guess they probably are better suited really.'

'Wow.' Sean shook his head. 'Your dad is a bit mad.'

'Yeah.' Michelle looked up at Sean. Her dad was mad. That was her shame, but Sean didn't seem horrified at all. She stood up and stepped towards him. Maybe Christmas was getting to her. 'Thank you.'

'What for?' His voice was quieter than normal, less certain.

'For persuading me to call him. And for letting me stay.'

'It's Ok.' Sean grinned. 'One more thing though?'

'What?' She could see the beginnings of more laughter in his eyes.

'Holly? They called you Holly.'

Now she could feel her cheeks reddening. 'It's my real first name.'

'And I'm guessing your dad picked it.'

She nodded. 'I hate it.'

'Why?'

'Jolly Holly! Prickly Holly! You must have been born at Christmas! Every boy wants a bit of Holly at Christmas!' She recited the familiar jibes from her youth. 'I could go on.'

'I like it.'

She shrugged.

'It's part of you.' Sean smiled. 'You can't change who you are.'

Maybe not, but for the first time in many years, Michelle thought maybe you could. Maybe you could be braver. Maybe you could take more chances. Maybe you could put what you wanted first. She took another step towards him. Sean stayed stock still, leaning on the wall behind the desk, watching her, breathing deep and slow. Michelle balled up her courage and took the final step, letting her fingertips move across his stomach. She felt his body tense. She tilted her face towards him and let her lips brush against his.

Relief flooded through her as he responded. Strong, safe arms encircled her and pulled her tight against his body.

Sean's tongue pushed against her mouth and she parted her lips, responding hungrily, instinctively to the feel and taste of him. His hand moved downwards and tugged at her jumper. Michelle raised her arms from around his neck and moved her body away from him a fraction, just enough for him to start to undress her. Sean flung the jumper to the corner of the room and wrapped her back into his arms. Michelle needed more. Lip against lip was intoxicating. She needed skin against skin. She pulled at his shirt, fumbling with buttons until he dragged it roughly over his head. She ran her fingers over his skin, feeling every hair, every bump through her fingertips. Her lips brushed his chest and she heard him sigh in response. She moved to his belt. Sean's hand clasped her wrist, slowing and stopping her.

She glanced up.

'Are you sure?'

She nodded.

Sean breathed deeply. 'We should probably talk . . . '

Michelle shook her head.

Sean closed his eyes for a second. 'I wanted to tell you about . . . '

She didn't want to talk. She didn't want to think about what the problems might be. Something was opening up inside her that she couldn't bear to see shut down. She needed to be close to him. 'Later.'

He nodded, and then all at once he was in control. He moved hungrily, desperately, in perfect time with her. They wrenched and tugged the rest of the clothes off each other's bodies, constantly touching and kissing, celebrating each new inch of undiscovered skin.

He lay her down on the rug at one

side of the room. The fur caressed her back, and she watched Sean lower himself to her side. She pulled him towards her, rolling him above her, wrapping herself around his hips.

'Wait.' Sean's voice was a low whisper.

Michelle's stomach clenched. He'd changed his mind. The cold familiar feeling of steel edged back into her gut. She sat up. 'What's wrong?'

Sean was rooting through the pocket of his jeans. 'What? Nothing. I . . . '

His voice tailed off as his fingers pulled a condom from the recesses of his wallet.

'Oh.' Relief bubbled from Michelle in a little nervous laugh. 'I thought you'd changed your mind.'

'No.' Sean's answer was instant and emphatic. 'Definitely no.'

Michelle lay back and watched him move across the room. Lean and strong, skin still tanned in the depths of winter from days and weeks working outside. He dragged a chair over to the study door and wedged it firmly closed. He grinned. 'Just in case.'

Michelle hadn't even thought of his family in the next room. 'Won't they wonder where we are?'

Sean shrugged. 'Probably won't even notice we're gone.'

Eventually, he came back to her. They moved more slowly now, taking their time, daring to start to believe in what was happening. He finally sank into her with one long easy stroke. She gasped. Her body tensed, holding him deep inside her.

'Ssshhhh,' he murmured.

She buried her face in his shoulder, lips pressed against his skin, breathing him in and out, muffling her moans from the house beyond. He made love to her. Slowly. Deeply. Sincerely. And then faster. Deeper. More urgent. More insistent.

Wave after wave of warmth streamed through Michelle's body as they came together, moaning and gasping against the other's sweat salted skin. He relaxed onto her for a second and she felt the weight, the utter solidity of him, before he rolled to the side.

'Wow.'

Michelle giggled. 'Yeah.'

Sean propped himself up on one elbow. 'Michelle?'

'Yeah.' She was still lying on her back, looking up at him now. Hopeful but uncertain. His body hadn't lied, she thought. He'd felt something and so had she. The word for that feeling hovered on the edge of her consciousness. She wasn't quite ready to let it in, but it was there insistently growing, ready to overwhelm her.

Sean opened his mouth. 'I do need to tell you about . . . '

A knock rattled the chair he'd wedged against the door. They both sat up. Another knock. Sean scrambled to his feet. There was a low clearing of the throat outside the door.

'Lunchtime,' called Sean's dad. 'Your mother asked me to come and find you.'

Michelle jumped up, grabbing her knickers from the desk where they'd been thrown earlier.

Sean stifled a laugh. 'We'll be there in a minute.'

They jostled round the room, picking up clothes, pulling them on hurriedly, without speaking. Michelle could feel her cheeks burning. What must Sean's family think of her? Turning up for Christmas with a man she'd only met a few days ago, and then disappearing to . . . to . . . erm . . . to have . . . her brain wouldn't allow her to think it aloud. She leant against the desk to pull her socks on, and then stood in the middle of the room smoothing down her jumper, unable to look at her . . . at her new . . . at Sean.

'Right then.' She started towards the door. Sean stepped behind her, grabbed her hand and spun her to face him.

'They can wait a minute longer.' He bent to kiss her, soft and strong and loaded with good intentions. Michelle responded, feeling her nerves settling.

Another knock.

Sean pulled away, resting his forehead onto hers. 'Once more unto the breach then Macduff.'

★ ★ ★

Christmas dinner in the Munro household was perfect in its imperfection. Gravy was spilt; siblings talked over one another; wine was spilt; children bickered over the last lonely pig-in-a-blanket; Sean's mum fretted about whether the turkey was cooked right through; her children reminded her, loudly, that she had the same panic every year and it was always, predictably, fine. Michelle was able to eat her meal quietly, squashed on one corner of the table, with Sean to one side, and the sharp tablecloth-covered drop to the children's table on the other.

She watched the family without her usual feeling of claustrophobia and discomfort. She'd hated family events with her dad and The Elf. She'd been shoehorned in, like they were trying to force her stiff, hard edges into a smooth, round hole. Here no one seemed to care where or how she fit; it was assumed that she would, and the family morphed and shifted around her to make space.

Listening to the chatter and eating her meal were small distractions from the thing taking up the rest of her attention. Sean. Sean, who was sitting right next to her. Sean, whose leg was brushing against her own. Sean, who was bending down to pick his dropped napkin from the floor and running his hand up her calf and thigh as he sat up again. Sean, whose mere proximity was making her senses tingle. Sean, who had finished his meal, and placed his hand, quietly, unobtrusively, hidden by the tablecloth, on her thigh where he was stroking small insistent circles, moving higher and higher.

Michelle gasped, and saw heads turn towards her. She covered quickly with a loud theatrical cough. Across the table, she could see the laughter in Bel's eye.

'You all right there?'

Michelle nodded. 'I'm good.'

# 6

## Christmas Afternoon, 2013

## Michelle

'Look who's here!'

Michelle looked up from an involved game of post-lunch Monopoly to see Bel ushering a stranger into the lounge. The newcomer was about Michelle's age, but that was their only point of similarity. This woman was radiantly beautiful, and exquisitely dressed. She pulled off her long wool coat to reveal leather boots below a fitted pencil skirt and soft silk blouse. The woman scanned the room before her gaze settled on Michelle.

'You're new.'

'Michelle is a . . . ' Bel paused. ' . . . a friend of Sean's.'

'Friend' sounded like a euphemism

for something sordid.

The newcomer smiled. 'How wonderful. I'm Cora.'

She stepped forward and leant to clasp Michelle's hand before Michelle could get up, leaving Michelle awkwardly half sitting and half standing.

'Sean and I go way back,' the newcomer continued. 'So many stories I could tell you about him.'

I bet there are, thought Michelle. She pulled her hand away and dragged herself to her feet. There was no mistaking the hint of fight in the stranger's tone, although it must have been clear that Michelle was not much opposition, stylish, as she was, in leggings and a borrowed Munro family Christmas jumper. She plastered on her most dazzling smile. 'Really? I'm not sure he's mentioned you.'

The woman paused, and pressed home her advantage. 'I wonder why not. You wouldn't think getting married would slip someone's mind, would you?'

Trying to pretend the thrust hadn't

hit a nerve, Michelle parried. 'Oh I knew that. I guess he must have forgotten to mention your name.'

Neither woman's smile faltered.

'Cora?' They both turned towards the doorway where Sean was standing. 'What are you doing here?'

Sean's mum bustled past her son, bustling any answer Cora might have offered away at the same time. 'Cora! Lovely to see you. Will you have a drink?'

Cora was hidden from view for a moment as Sean's mother, then father and niece and nephew, enveloped her in hugs and welcomes. Michelle was isolated. Sean was still hovering in the doorway, but everyone else was treating Cora like visiting royalty. However friendly they might be, Michelle reminded herself, she wasn't part of this family. She was an outsider. They'd made her feel welcome, but it was nothing more than a feeling. Michelle knew better than to rely on those.

Cora disentangled herself from the hugs. 'Chloe, why don't you take a look in the hallway? There's a bag you might be interested in.'

The twins dashed into the hallway and re-appeared dragging a bulging sack of presents. Cora waved a manicured hand. 'Well, you can't come visiting at Christmas empty-handed, now can you?'

Presents were pulled out of the sack and handed round. Cora sat herself down in the centre of the sofa.

The group redrew itself around her. Extravagant gifts were opened. Drinks were offered and accepted. It was the picture of the perfect Christmas scene, except in Michelle's heart. It was true. Sean had a wife, and she wasn't imaginary or far away or hideously disfigured and only able to eat through a straw. She was real and here and hideously beautiful and put together. Michelle wanted to run, but she was trapped in this house until at least the following morning. Even if she tried to leave now, she had no way of getting back to civilisation, unless . . .

'Anyway, darling, I do need a quick word with you.' Cora was talking to Sean who was still hanging back near the door.

He nodded and the couple walked out into the hall.

★　★　★

Sean led the way into the study and closed the door.

'What are you doing here?'

'I came to see you. It's Christmas.' She slinked across the room towards him, smiling her perfect lipsticked smile. 'I texted.'

'Well, you've seen me.'

She pouted. 'Why so hostile? I thought after I let you use the flat, we might be back on better terms.'

Sean took a breath. 'We're on fine terms. I appreciate the use of the flat, but you asked me. You said it would help you out to have someone housesitting. I could just as easily have got a hotel.'

Another pout. 'So businesslike. You didn't used to be so businesslike.'

That stuck in his throat. 'And isn't that why you left me? You wanted someone with a bit more ambition.'

She perched on the edge of the desk. 'But then you turned out all ambitious. There was a piece about you in Scottish Life you know.'

'I know.'

'Apparently, you're an eligible bachelor.'

Sean didn't respond.

'So why don't we?'

'What?'

'You know.' She was being coy now, but Sean knew what was coming. 'We were always great together. We could rekindle?'

She stood up and moved right in front of him. 'I always turned you on, didn't I? We never had any problems in that department. And you loved me, didn't you?'

'Yeah.' Sean couldn't stop the tiny nod of his head.

'So you and me? It always worked.'

Sean was distracted for a second by a sound in the hallway. He moved past Cora to the door and looked out. There was no one there. He closed the door again and leant against the frame.

'It didn't always work, Cora. We got divorced.'

She stuck out her bottom lip.

Sean closed his eyes. 'You've got to stop doing this. We can't keep going back.'

'It's not just me.'

It was true. There were plenty of times in the past decade when he'd met up with Cora for a drink, to clear the air, just as friends, and ended up falling back into the pattern, back into her bed, but it wasn't real. 'I know, but it's got to stop. Neither of us is happy. Neither of us is moving on.'

'Is this because of that ginger girl?'

'Not just her.'

'I miss you.' She was wheedling now, not accepting that she was beaten, trying to get around him.

'Then you shouldn't have left.' As he said the words Sean realised that it really could be that simple. 'But you did, a long time ago.'

Cora took a step away from him and shook out her hair. She arranged her face into a smile. 'No need to be grumpy. I'm only messing around.' Sean didn't answer, allowing her to save face.

'Best get back to the olds then.'

Sean nodded. 'Give them my love.'

He walked her to the door and they stopped, unsure how to say goodbye. A kiss on the cheek? A hug? A shake of the hand? In the end she just left.

A few minutes earlier, Michelle had darted away from the study door as she heard Sean's footsteps come towards her. She pressed herself against the wall, out of sight, as he glanced to see who was in the hallway, before closing the door and going back to the tête-à-tête with his wife.

Michelle breathed through the wave of nausea that hit her. They were going to get back together. She wasn't just betrayed; she was humiliated, and it was her own fault. She'd had years to learn not to trust a man who treated life like a game. She put her hand against the wall to steady herself. Sean's perfect wife wanted her perfect life back. There was no way Michelle could stand in the way of that. She wasn't even the wronged party here. She wasn't her mother. She was The Elf.

She swallowed as hard as she could, trying to force her lunch to stay where it was. There was a table at the end of the hallway. She saw a set of keys lying amongst the discarded gloves and junk mail. She grabbed them.

'Are you off somewhere?'

Sean's dad was standing behind her.

'I . . . I've got a friend who lives quite near. I thought I'd pop and visit. You know, as it's Christmas.'

'Aye.'

'Right.' Michelle picked up the car keys and fled the house. She had no idea where she was going, but she had to get away. She couldn't watch the happy couple being reunited. She jumped into the hire car and drove out of the yard. She followed roads at random, driving too fast, brain flitting in every direction and landing on one single thought. What if she was wrong?

She moved her foot to the brake to slow down. She felt the car slide beneath her. She slammed her foot hard on the brake, cursing herself at the same time. 'Never brake into a skid,' she heard the voice of her geriatric driving instructor in her head. Too late.

## Christmas Day, 1992

We're having something called fajitas. I made Auntie Barbara write it down for me. It is written f-a-j-i-t-a, but you say it fa-heeeee-ta. Auntie Barbara says it is from Mexico, which is a special type of Spain. Auntie Barbara isn't staying for lunch. She said there was plenty of turkey for us at her house, but Mummy said that she wasn't in the mood for all that business.

Then they went in the kitchen and talked in quiet voices but I could still hear them because Dolly wanted to play in the hallway so I had to go with her. Dolly sometimes does things like that. She is much braver than I am.

'It's not right for a child at Christmas.'

Mummy doesn't answer that.

'I mean, I understand why you're not feeling like it this year, but come on.'

Mummy laughs. 'I'm sure they'll have the full spread tomorrow at her father's.'

I'm having a different Christmas just with Daddy tomorrow. When we came back here from Auntie Barbara's house I thought it might be so we could all see Daddy for Christmas, but Mummy says that Daddy doesn't live here any more, and this house is just mine and hers now. Mine and hers and Dolly's.

They've forgotten that they're talking quietly now, and Mummy starts to shout at Auntie Barbara. I tell Dolly that I think we should play in the lounge. There's a spot in between the sofa and Mummy's sewing box where I can squeeze right in, with Dolly, and make myself small. I squash into my spot and sing *Away in a Manger*. Last year Mummy and me sang Christmas carols together before bed on Christmas Eve. She didn't want to do that this year.

I'm going to make sure Mummy has a lovely Christmas. When my fajitas come, I'm going to eat them all up and make 'Mmmm' noises even though they've got yellow bits in them, and I don't know what they are. Dolly doesn't like yellow bits. She might leave hers on the side of the plate.

'Are you having a nice day dear?' Mummy asks.

'Yeah.'

'Good.' She seems pleased. 'Christmas is a bit of silliness really. It's much nicer this way, isn't it?'

I nod. I think that's what she wants me to do.

# 7

## Christmas Afternoon, 2013

### Sean

Sean watched Cora stalk back to her car, and headed back into the lounge. 'Where's Michelle?'

Bel looked up from the Monopoly board. 'She's gone. She said she had friends to visit.'

What? That made no sense. Michelle didn't know anyone around here. It didn't matter. All that mattered was that she had gone.

'When?'

Bel shrugged. 'Ten minutes ago maybe.'

'Did she say anything?'

A shake of the head. 'No.'

Sean ran into the yard. The hire car, as he expected, was gone. He quickly counted back through the day. Coffee at breakfast time, even though his mum and Bel seemed to have been quaffing Buck's Fizz from first light. One glass of wine with lunch. That was Ok. He ran back into the house.

'Car keys!'

'What?' His parents, brother and sister all stared at him. 'I need to borrow someone's car. Any car!'

He caught the first set of keys that came flying towards him and ran outside pressing the unlock button. Luke's Land Rover sprang into life. Thank the Lord. He'd said any car, but he was relieved not to be chasing the woman of his dreams in his mother's bright yellow smart car. He started the engine, pulled away and immediately stopped. Which way had she gone? He silently thanked the Lord again, this time for the snow, and for the fact that Christmas Day meant there weren't many tracks coming in and out of the yard. He could see footsteps, presumably Cora's, going off across the field.

He could see where his dad had brought the hire car back, but those tracks were already part covered in fresh snow. He turned out of the yard, following the newest tyre marks.

This was crazy. He could wait until after Christmas, get her contact details from Patrick and Jess, give her a call sometime calm and quiet. He could be sensible. He could take things slow. He didn't have to dive straight in. Sean grinned to himself, pressed his foot to the clutch and moved up a gear.

He followed the lane from the farm for about a mile, to the crossroads. The lack of Christmas Day traffic meant that even out on the road there were only a few tyre tracks. The freshest seemed to go straight on. He followed them.

The lane rose and fell with the landscape, and then started to rise more sharply as the road climbed into the higher hills. Sean glanced at the sky. The fresh snow was falling more heavily, and the snow on the ground was getting thicker as he climbed higher. Would the hire car make it through this? He shuddered to think of Michelle alone and probably lost.

He rounded a bend, and brought the Land Rover to a rapid stop. The hire car was half off the road in front of him, nose into the ditch. He threw his door open and ran. The front of the car was crumpled, but the car was empty. The driver's side door was open. He spun around scanning the road and fields. No Michelle.

His heart pounded. Where was she? Was she hurt? Cold? Out there somewhere alone? He imagined the landscape he loved through Michelle's eyes. Freezing. Forbidding. Dangerous. He ran back to the four by four and opened the boot. Good old Luke. You could always spot a boy who'd been brought up on a farm. There was a waterproof jacket, along with a shovel and first aid kit. Sean pulled on the coat, and headed back to the hire car. He dragged his phone out of his pocket.

No signal. He hadn't thought there would be. No sign of Michelle in or near the car. No key in the ignition. He tried to tell himself that was a good thing. It looked like she'd got out and walked away. Steeling himself, he ran his hands over the steering wheel and driver's seat. No obvious signs of blood.

'Sean!'

He spun round to see Michelle standing in the lane. There was blood on her hand, but she was standing and breathing and talking. His heart rate started to slow. He ran towards her.

'You're Ok?'

She nodded. 'What are you doing out here?'

'Looking for you.'

He saw her open expression snap closed. 'That's not necessary. I'm . . . '

'If you're going to say 'fine' then I'm going to point out the car in the ditch and the blood on your arm. You're not fine. You need help.'

She nodded but made no attempt to move towards him.

'I'm sorry if you don't want my help, but I'm all that's here, so sit down.'

He flicked the tailgate open, and gestured towards it. Michelle sat down while Sean leant into the car and dragged a first aid kit from the glove box.

'Roll up your sleeve.'

The cut was on the back of her wrist and wasn't as bad as Sean had first feared. He found an antiseptic wipe and started to clean.

'I can do that.' Michelle took the wipe off him with her good hand and started to deal with her own wound.

'Why did you run off?'

Michelle shrugged. 'It seemed perfectly clear that I wasn't wanted.'

'What?'

Michelle swallowed, still holding the wipe against her arm. 'Look. I'm sure you were trying to be nice, and this probably isn't your fault but I don't do things like this. I don't ride Ferris wheels. I don't play in the snow. I don't run away with strange men. I don't . . . '

She tailed off, as if the other things she didn't do were too numerous to list.

Sean laughed, trying to keep the tone lighter than he felt. 'You do now.'

'No. I don't.' Michelle lifted the wipe from her wrist. 'I need to put something on this.'

Sean accepted the distraction. 'I don't think there's a plaster big enough.' He fished around in the first aid kit.

'Hold this.' He pressed a pad against the cut, and started wrapping a piece of bandage to hold it in place. 'I thought there was something good happening here.'

Her face was pinched and closed, like it had been when he'd first met her, like it had been before he'd persuaded her to ride the Ferris wheel, and shown her the Christmas tree field. She wouldn't look him in the eye. 'Apparently not.'

Sean swallowed. 'What happened?'

She glared at him. 'Seriously? I thought . . . it doesn't matter.'

'You thought what?'

'I thought you might, sort of, want to . . . '

Sean smiled. 'I did. I do. I very much sort of, want to . . . '

'Well that's not going to happen.' She took a breath. 'Well not again.'

Sean paused in his bandage wrapping. What had happened? Things had been going well. Things had been going really well. 'Help me here. I'm confused.'

Michelle pulled her hand away. 'What's confusing? You had a bit of fun. It didn't work out.'

'What?'

She set off walking back along the lane. He ran after her. 'Seriously. I'm getting really tired of watching you walk away.'

'Then why don't you let me go?'

'Because I don't want to.' He yelled his answer back at her, and the shouting was exhilarating. 'Because I'm sick of being cautious and sensible. Because I want to jump in with both feet, and I don't care if I get hurt.'

'You don't care about getting hurt?'

'Not even a little bit. I think you might be worth it.'

Michelle let out a small bitter laugh. 'And what do you reckon your wife would think?'

'What?'

'Your wife?'

Oh. Sean was stupid. Cora. Of course she'd have told a possible rival she was his wife. That was exactly what she'd do. He took a deep breath. 'Look. I can explain.'

'I'm not interested.'

'I tried to tell you before we . . . before we did anything. You didn't want to wait.'

'How long would it have taken to mention your wife?'

'She's not my wife.'

Michelle was still striding away from him.

He tried another tack. 'You can't walk anywhere from here. It's freezing. I know, for a fact, that that's not your jumper, so you have to take it back.

209

Come on. You don't even know where you are.'

She stuck out her chin. 'I do.'

'Where?'

Her chin lowered. 'Scotland.'

'Excellent. Well I'm sure that's all you'll need to tell the AA for them to pop out here on Christmas Day and pick you up.' He saw her shoulders drop. 'Come back to the Land Rover. Let me explain.'

She walked past him without speaking, and sat back down on the tailgate. 'Two minutes.'

Two minutes. What could you explain in two minutes? The big stuff, he guessed. If you were going to jump right in, you couldn't be half-hearted about it. 'I'm not married.'

She raised her eyes.

'I was married. I'm divorced. I should have told you that. I tried to tell you that.'

She folded her arms across her chest. 'So tell me about it now.'

'Ok.' What to say? 'It was a long time

ago. We were seventeen. We were in love. I leapt right in, didn't think, didn't hesitate. I wanted to be with her.'

'What went wrong?'

He looked at her. 'Apart from being seventeen?'

She laughed, a small quiet laugh. It was beautiful.

'We stayed together quite a while actually, living with my mum and dad. Then, when she was twenty-one, she started thinking about all the stuff she'd missed out on. University. Wild nights out. Growing up, I guess.'

'And that's why you broke up?'

'She didn't tell me until she already had the place at college. One day I thought we were fine. The next she was moving to London to do Business and Economics, and I wasn't invited.'

He closed his eyes.

'I'm sorry.'

'I haven't really jumped into a relationship since then.'

'Once bitten?'

Sean nodded.

'Are you still in love with her?'

'What?'

'I heard you talking at the house.'

'I knew there was someone in the hall!' He paused and shook his head.

'How do you know?'

'I know.' He turned to face her. 'Honestly. I'm not in love with Cora. She's cool in her own slightly self-involved way. We have history, but I think I've been kidding myself that we can be mates. She's part of my past. That's all.'

Michelle didn't answer.

'So what about the future?'

'What?'

Sean leant towards her. 'Well, officially you still owe me another twenty-four hours.'

Michelle shook her head. 'That was always a silly idea.'

'I know.' Sean swallowed. He was all in now. No pretending this was just him taking pity on a girl who was alone at Christmas. No pretending that when the two days were over he'd be able to stand by and let her walk away. 'I was kidding myself about the forty-eight hour thing as well. I don't want a couple of days with you. It's not enough. I don't want to be safe. I don't want a time limit. I want to take care of you. I want to spend time with you. I want . . . I just want you.'

Michelle kept her head bent away from him as she spoke. 'I don't think I can do that.'

'Do what?'

'Jump right in. What if it doesn't work? What if I've seen this whole relationship play out before?'

'What do you mean?'

'My mum and dad. He was so impulsive, so much fun, and she was like me. Careful. Cautious. It didn't work for them.' She lifted her head towards Sean. 'Why would it work for us?'

That was it. That was her biggest fear. She'd loved her dad so much, but he'd let her mum down. He'd let them both down. 'Well, for starters, I'm not like your dad. Yes. I'm a bit impulsive, but I don't quit. I'm not going to run off with an elf . . . '

Michelle opened her mouth, but Sean kept going.

' . . . or a secretary or my ex-wife or a foxy Christmas tree saleswoman or whoever it is you're worrying about. When you're around, I don't see anyone else. I only see you. I see you taking care of everybody, and I want to take care of you.'

Michelle shook her head again. 'You'll get bored of me. Sensible Michelle.'

'There's nothing boring about sensible Michelle.' Sean grinned. 'And if I get bored of sensible Michelle, I've always got Holly.'

'Shut up!' The hint of a smile was returning to Michelle's voice.

'And so what if you are your mother's daughter? Your mother's dying wish was that you went on holiday to the Caribbean. That's hardly sensible.'

Michelle sighed. 'I suppose not. I

think maybe she thought she'd stopped me having fun when I was younger.'

'So maybe you're both your parents? Sensible Michelle and impulsive Holly?'

'Maybe. Actually, when I was little I had a dolly, called Dolly . . . '

Sean grinned. 'What else?'

'I used to make her do the things I was too scared to do.' She smiled at the memory. 'Like I had to be Michelle but she could be Holly in my place.'

She shook her head. It was a silly idea. 'You could still break my heart. My dad broke Mum's heart.'

Sean shrugged. 'And you could break mine.'

'I wouldn't do that.'

'Good.' He took a deep breath. 'One question then, when we're together, do you see anyone else?'

Did she? She paused for a second. Normally her head was full of plans and things to do and problems to solve, but the last twenty-four hours had been different. She'd managed, mostly, to just be in the here and now, because the here and now with Sean in the middle of it had been all she could see. Michelle shook her head. 'It's just you.'

Sean leant towards her and she found his lips. Soft, chilled from the cold air, intoxicating but safe. Maybe she could trust a feeling. Maybe she could jump into the unknown and let him catch her. She kissed him back.

She pulled back a fraction. 'I crashed your hire car.'

'Yep.'

'What are we going to do?'

'Dunno.' He glanced at the car in the ditch. 'I can probably tow it back somehow. Don't worry about it today. It's Christmas.'

'Oh.' She sounded sad.

'What's up?'

'It's getting dark. Christmas is nearly over.'

'I thought you hated Christmas.'

'Maybe I'm a convert.'

Sean laughed. 'Well, in that case, can I interest you in New Year?'

'What?'

'Well, this is Scotland. Really Hogmanay is what it's all about. We'll go to Edinburgh.'

She squirmed. 'I don't know. Isn't New Year a big waste of money?'

Sean shook his head. 'I'll do you a deal. Give me another week. I'll get you to love New Year. I promise.'

'Just one week?'

'Well, a week until New Year.' He pulled her closer. 'After that, we can start planning next Christmas.'

We do hope that you have enjoyed reading this large print book.

Did you know that all of our titles are available for purchase?

We publish a wide range of high quality large print books including:
**Romances, Mysteries, Classics General Fiction Non Fiction and Westerns**

Special interest titles available in large print are:
**The Little Oxford Dictionary Music Book, Song Book Hymn Book, Service Book**

Also available from us courtesy of Oxford University Press:
**Young Readers' Dictionary (large print edition) Young Readers' Thesaurus (large print edition)**

For further information or a free brochure, please contact us at:
**Ulverscroft Large Print Books Ltd., The Green, Bradgate Road, Anstey, Leicester, LE7 7FU, England. Tel:** (00 44) **0116 236 4325 Fax:** (00 44) **0116 234 0205**

# WHAT HAPPENS IN NASHVILLE

## Angela Britnell

Claire Buchan is hardly over the moon about travelling to Nashville, Tennessee for her sister's hen party: a week of honky-tonks, karaoke and cowboys. Certainly not strait-laced Claire's idea of a good time, what with her lawyer job and sensible boyfriend, Philip. But then she doesn't bank on meeting Rafe Cavanna. On the surface, Rafe fits the cowboy stereotype, with his handsome looks and roguish charm. But as he and Claire get to know each other, she realises there is far more to him than meets the eye . . .

# GRAND DESIGNS

## Linda Mitchelmore

Interior decorator Carrie Fraser cannot believe her luck when she is invited to work at beautiful Oakenbury Hall. Nor can she quite get over the owner of the Hall, the gorgeous and wealthy Morgan Harrington. Morgan is bound by his late father's wishes to keep Oakenbury within the family and have children; and the more time Carrie spends with him, the more she yearns to be the woman to fulfil this wish. But the likes of Carrie Fraser could never be enough for a high-flying businessman like Morgan . . . could she?

# A WESTERN HEART

## Liz Harris

Wyoming, 1880: Childhood sweethearts Rose McKinley and Will Hyde have always been destined to marry; and with their parents just as keen on the match, there is nothing to stop them. Except perhaps Cora, Rose's younger sister. Lovesick and hung up on Will, she is fed up with the happy couple. So when the handsome Mr Galloway comes to town and turns Rose's head, Cora sees an opportunity to get what she wants: Will . . .

# MARRY FOR LOVE

## Christina Courtenay

Delilah cannot bear to watch as her twin sister Deborah marries Hamish Baillie, fourth earl of Blackwood. Not only because she knows that Deborah has manipulated him into marriage, but also because she herself has been in love with Hamish since she first set eyes on him. When Delilah makes the ultimate sacrifice to save Hamish from her sister's clutches, he is grateful — but he can't help but be suspicious of her motives. And her scheming twin is not going to let go of the Earl that easily . . .